DESERT FLAME

Romy, a make-up artist with a company filming a commercial in Egypt, was shocked to learn that her ex-fiancé, Alex, had become the director. Alex was convinced that Romy still loved him and continued to pursue her. Romy also had to contend with passes from Shane, a handsome male model, but she didn't think he was right for her. She much preferred Martin, but he was so very shy. It was only when she became involved in a kidnapping that Romy discovered where her feelings really lay.

Books by Joy St. Clair
in the Linford Romance Library:

EDGE OF ECSTASY
INTIMATE JOURNEY
HEART IN THE CLOUDS
A KISS TO REMEMBER

JOY ST. CLAIR

DESERT FLAME

Complete and Unabridged

LINFORD
Leicester

First published in Great Britain in 1998

First Linford Edition
published 1998

British Library CIP Data

St. Clair, Joy
Desert flame.—Large print ed.—
Linford romance library
1. Love stories
2. Large type books
I. Title
823.9′14 [F]

ISBN 0–7089–5260–7

Published by
F. A. Thorpe (Publishing) Ltd.
Anstey, Leicestershire

Set by Words & Graphics Ltd.
Anstey, Leicestershire
Printed and bound in Great Britain by
T. J. International Ltd., Padstow, Cornwall

This book is printed on acid-free paper

1

ROMY searched her voluminous holdall for a kohl pencil.

"I know it's in here somewhere," she wailed. "Goodness! This is ridiculous."

"Oh, do stop fiddling in that bag. You're like an old witch with all your powders and potions," moaned Decima, never in the best of moods at six o'clock in the morning, but unusually irritable today. "I'm fed up with this place. I hate the climate, it's so hot and sticky. And I hate the sand. It's all gritty and gets in everywhere. And I hate my face being all greasy like this. I just know I'm going to get spots."

"Sorry, love, if I'm getting on your nerves," said Romy, sounding quite unrepentant. "Your skin is too fair for you to be a natural daughter of the Nile. I've got my orders to turn you into a Cleopatra look-alike and that's exactly what I'm going to do." She grinned. "Fear not! You won't get any spots, not from my make-up." And with a triumphant shout she held aloft the elusive kohl pencil.

Decima scowled at her reflection in the large oval mirror balanced on top of the travelling trunk which was serving as a makeshift dressing table. "Why did I ever think modelling was a glamorous career? I thought I had it made when I was chosen to be the *Rabbion* girl. It was such a big thing. The press were onto it in a flash, they all thought it so marvellous. I was really conned." She gave an exaggerated sigh. "What I'd give to be back stacking shelves at Tesco's." Her eyes grew dreamy for a moment. "Do you know what I would like right now? A large lager with lots of ice."

"Oh, no you don't," muttered Romy. "If you think I'm going to do your mouth again you've got another think coming." She skilfully applied the kohl pencil to the model's eyelids and blended in the colour with her fingertips. "It's all right for you. You've only got one scene to do then you can go back to the hotel and wallow by that gorgeous pool. I've got to be here all day ready with the touch-up sponge. Do you know? I haven't seen our hotel in daylight yet."

There came a sound of someone clearing his throat outside. "Are you decent?" Kieron poked his head round the tent flap and, seeing Decima wore a make-up shift, entered to peer critically at her reflection.

"Ye-es," he said slowly, his boyish features breaking into a grin of approval. "Perhaps a little more blusher, Romy."

"As you wish," said Romy blithely. "You're the director." Another burrow in the holdall produced a handful of blushers.

As Kieron moved to look over her shoulder he stood very near to her and she could feel his hot breath on her cheek. Kieron was all right, a happily married man, and she thanked her lucky stars he wasn't Alex. The mere thought of her ex-fiancé served to make her pulses race and her legs turn to jelly.

Alex was a first-class director, acknowledged as one of the best, and she should have been professional enough to set aside her personal prejudices, but after she had broken up with him she had sworn never to work with him again.

She wished she hadn't started thinking about Alex because now she couldn't stop and for a moment she was reminded of all the old longing.

She'd been completely under his spell. He had used her to boost his ego — not that it needed a boost considering how successful he was in his chosen profession — and she had been a willing slave. But not any more. Her eyes had been opened and there was only so far she could go in deluding herself. She had vowed not to be so foolish again.

He'd been too bossy, too possessive, and thought he owned her very soul. She had been flattered at first, his wanting to know where she had been when she wasn't with him, but it had got tedious, having to account for her every moment. Then he had started telling her what to wear, what to do and what to think even.

She might have gone on imagining herself in love with him if it had not been for one terrible weekend when he had made her change all her plans just because she would be out of his sight. She had suddenly realised that he didn't love her, he only wanted someone to own who would adore him. She could go on being his doormat for as long as he ordained or she could make a clean break of it and get out while she still had some vestige of pride left.

She chose to get out.

It hadn't been easy. He was loath to let her go — she had been good for him, his own built-in admiration clapometer She hadn't envisaged he would turn nasty. She couldn't believe how nasty, calling her all the names under the sun, and she had escaped to sob her heart out. He had ruined her life for she was sure she would never be able to love like that again.

For a while she had wondered if she had done the right thing. And having to live through the lonely days thinking about his passionate kisses and the feel of his arms about her was almost too much to bear. Frankly his absence wreaked havoc on her nerves.

She had loved everything about him, the way he walked, the looseness of limbs which gave him a rolling sort of gait. She loved the way he laughed, which was often, throwing back his blond head and letting out an infectious guffaw.

She loved the way he would think up ways to please and surprise her, like the time of the Valentine's Day dance when he had rented the banner down the hall at the community centre to proclaim his love for her. ROMY IS THE GIRL FOR ALEX it had said in gold letters two feet high. And there was the time when on her birthday he had persuaded her mother to let him into the house to fill the bath to the brim with flowers.

He had made her feel special as no-one had before. Or since.

"Good for you, Romy," her friends had said after the break. "We wondered how long you were going to let him walk all over you."

But knowing she was well rid of him didn't begin to make up for the bitter taste of loss. His going had left a void in her life which she never expected to fill. Although she was aware she was incapable of loving again with such intensity, Alex couldn't hurt her now if he tried. But to be on the safe side she had put in for a transfer to Kieron's unit. She had grown strong in the four months they had been apart.

"Ow!" It was a cry of pain from

Decima and Romy saw she had inadvertently flicked the brush in her eye. She hastily reached for a paper towel but Decima pushed her hand away.

"Get away! You've done enough damage for one morning. I don't know what's got into you." She leaned forward to study her reflection once more and made a disparaging noise with her tongue against her teeth. "Do you know what's the matter with her, Kieron? Man trouble, I suppose."

Romy knew Decima wasn't being bitchy, she didn't know of her broken heart, no-one did in this unit. And she meant to keep it that way. She didn't want anyone's pity, she just wanted to be left alone to get over it in her own way.

She emptied the holdall carefully onto the dressing table and tried to bring some order to its contents as she replaced them.

A week after she had told him goodbye, Alex had called at the house, confident he could win her back. He had used all his charm, sending her a taxi-load of heart-shaped balloons; having her name broadcast over the BBC loudspeakers; hiring a guitarist to play love songs underneath her window. But all she could think was how he wanted his own way all the time.

Kieron lifted the flap and ducked out of the tent and Romy turned her head in order to hide the tears that were trembling in her eyes. She should be over Alex by now and have found someone else. But there was no-one who remotely interested her. She was destined for a lonely loveless life.

She picked up the short black wig which would hide Decima's fiery hair and gave it a fierce brushing.

"Hey. Steady on! You'll turn it bald." Decima glowered at it. "That thing's so hot. I hate it." And she gave a groan.

"I know," sympathised Romy. "But I won't put it on you till the very last minute."

"No, I know you won't." Decima sounded a little calmer. "You're a good sort. You seem to be a natural for your job."

"Well, thanks."

For as long as she could remember Romy had wanted to be a make-up artist She had left technical college at eighteen with the necessary qualifications — A levels in English and Art and an O level in history — and taken a two-year course in hairdressing and beauty culture. This had been enough to get her a place on a BBC Make-Up Training Scheme and she had loved ever moment of it. She had learnt so much and eventually emerged as a senior make-up artist.

Her first job had been working in the light entertainment department of the BBC, making wigs and false noses and suchlike. She had done well and emerged feeling confident about the future.

She could hardly believe her good luck whenm after trying for only six months, she had landed the highly-sought-after job with this famous advertising agency, The Blue Ribbon Associates.

Alex came with the package she discovered and she was delirious when he singled her out for special attention. After she had broken off their engagement it was as if the bottom had dropped out of her world. But she should have known better. Goodness! She was twenty-two and Alex hadn't been the first man in her life. She must have been very naive. Not any more, she'd learned her lesson — the hard way. It would be a long time before she trusted a man again. Any man.

She saw Decima watching her in the mirror reflection, a look of exasperation on her lovely face, as if she was waiting for an answer.

"I'm sorry," said Romy. "I was miles away."

"Yes, weren't you?" Decima pursed her lips into a tight knot. "Look. I said, are you going to help get me into this costume or aren't you? I know it isn't strictly your department but there's no-one else." She held up the silvery-blue chiffon material which had been scantily made into a kind of harem tunic. "It's a devil of a job to put on. I'm scared of putting my fingers through it."

Romy reached for it. "All right, I'll help. Brace yourself."

It called for a delicate touch but between them they managed to ease it over the model's slim curves.

"You look stunning," declared Romy sincerely.

"Thanks." Decima was used to compliments and took them as her due. She wasn't exactly the stereotyped dumb beauty but she came close and Romy had learned it was no use discussing anything other than men and shopping with her, not if she wanted a sensible answer.

Decima went to the flap of the tent and gazed out at the undulating sand dunes beyond which could just be glimpsed the top of the Great Pyramid. "I've never been to Egypt before," she murmured broodingly. "I always pictured it as a romantic place, not a boring endless desert."

Romy protested, "It's not all desert. We just happen to be in the Sahara. They say Cairo is very nice — if we ever get a chance to see it. As I was saying before, all I've seen of it yet is a view from my hotel window. That's what comes from getting up at the crack of dawn and being driven out here before it's properly light."

Decima looked troubled for a moment. Then she just sat there biting the inside of her mouth.

"What's the matter?" enquired Romy gently. "You look as if you've all the trouble in the world."

"I'm dead scared of those camels," replied the model. "They smell awful, don't they? I needed a long soak after only two minutes on one yesterday."

"Yes, they do pong," agreed Romy, "But they've got handlers. You'll be all right." Head on one side, she studied the other critically. "I think that hem is a bit wonky. I'd better stitch it for you. Won't be a tick."

She went behind the mirror to open the trunk and took out needle and cotton, breaking a length of the latter off with her teeth and threading it.

Falling to her knees, she said, "Yes, I don't envy you having to ride on one of those contrary beasts."

Decima grabbed Romy's arm and her expression was one of sheer terror now. "Oh Romy, they really do frighten me. I wish I'd never agreed to do this. What's so special about being the *Rabbion* girl, anyway? Who else is crazy enough to want to be her?"

As Romy got to her feet, she hid a grin, while her pale blue eyes sparkled. "Only every model in the world."

"Okay, so the pay is fantastic. But I earn every penny of it." Decima pulled a face. "If I'm not sinking in a swamp or falling over a cliff. I'm being nibbled at by nasty little piranha fish. Why does everything have to be real? Haven't they heard of cardboard cut-outs?"

Romy smiled wryly as she helped Decima on with a satin housecoat the colour of warm honey which enhanced the natural redness of her hair giving it a warm glow. "They pride themselves on authenticity. There's a great deal of money involved and . . . "

"I know," interrupted Decima. "Money talks."

In fact it cost less using the real locations, Romy mused. To make a mock-up of this scene in the desert would cost the earth, to say nothing of the expense involved in finding genuine-looking extras And then there was the atmosphere. You couldn't skimp on that.

Decima forced a grin. "Oh, don't listen to me. I must have got out of bed the wrong side this morning."

Kieron appeared in the tent opening again. He was the perfect gentleman with his public school accent and old-world manners. “Are you ready, Decima? The light’s perfect.” He looked thoughtful. “I never knew the desert could be so beautiful, but the colours of the sky this morning have been an eye-opener. I would like to do more work here.”

Decima made a sour face only Romy could see. “That makes one of us then.”

They both went out and Martin appeared in the tent entrance. He hesitated for a brief spell and then asked Romy, “Are you ready for me yet?”

“Take a pew,” she said, “I’ll be with you in a moment.” She turned to the water barrel and rinsed out her brushes before placing them in the mobile sterilizer.

She said brightly, “I hear you’re riding a camel today.”

“Yeah!”

Martin was the stuntman. Anything dangerous and he stood in for the *Rabbion* man.

She liked him. He had none of the arrogance that the models had although he was very good-looking, with a mop of nutbrown hair that took some taming, and a marvellous physique. She considered he had by far the most unpleasant and difficult job, but he wasn't given to complaining. In fact he was rather shy.

He eased his long legs round the cabin trunk. "I've never had anything to do with camels. I only hope Mustapha can handle them. They're cussed beasts apparently."

"Rather you than me." Romy tied a smock around his neck. She had to disguise his features so that he appeared anonymous and it involved spreading on thick matt make-up.

"What are you doing this evening?" he asked. "Would you let me buy you a drink?" His smoky grey eyes were anxious for a moment before he glanced away.

She smiled to herself. He had been working up to it since they arrived two days ago. She had wondered how she could help him and decided she couldn't. He would have to do it in his own sweet way. Here was another perfect gentleman with manners of which she approved.

"I'd be delighted to have a drink with you," she answered in like manner. "Where shall we meet? I mean in which bar?"

She was busy working on his mouth which prevented him from speaking.

He waited until she had finished and said, "Better make it the Sheba Bar. It's a great hotel they've put us in, isn't it?"

Romy agreed. The superior accommodation was one of the perks of the job.

She finished working on him and he departed, giving her time for a breather. All she wore was a cotton smock over her bra and panties but she was still hot.

She pulled off her white turban-like hat which she wore to keep her long hair out of the way when she was working. She had seriously considered having it cut for this climate, but didn't want to lose her tresses after she had taken so long to grow them. She ruffled her fair locks with her fingers, bending over to allow the air to circulate.

She heard a low whistle and straightened to see Shane Shelley regarding her in his usual provocative manner.

No polite clearing of the throat for Shane. He came right in. "Hello, Romy, my darling," he greeted her, flopping down on a wooden bench. "And how's my favourite make-up lady today? Well, I hope."

"Hi! Shane. I'm fine, if you don't count the heat." She hastily piled her hair on top of her head and stuffed it back into the turban, grinning as she motioned him to the canvas chair recently vacated by Martin.

He chuckled. "It's a crying shame to hide all that glorious hair under a turban."

"We're working on you, not me."

He gazed up at her, a glint of self-mockery in his eyes. "You're wasting your time then. Unless you think you can improve on nature." When she did not answer he took her hand and said, "Well, do you?"

Still she refused to feed his ego and as she gently but firmly freed herself from his grasp, marvelled, not for the first time, at his conceit.

Shane Shelley was the *Rabbion* man and he certainly looked the part. A handsome specimen of manhood, he was well over six feet tall without an ounce of surplus flesh on his bones.

Romy considered all models were posers, he especially. He was reputed to have turned many a top model girl's head. His hair, cut longish to just above his shoulders, was as black as coal and Romy, because of her profession, knew it was the colour nature had bestowed on him. That wasn't all she had generously endowed him with. His eyes were green, but no ordinary green, these were a kind of shamrock green one moment and a deep, sea green the next. Romy had never seen such eyes. His cheekbones were sharp and sculpted and he could have been taken for a Greek god but for a scar that ran down the crease at the side of his nose. He was proud of that scar. He had earned it fighting off a mugger in Hyde Park, he told anyone who would listen. He was right about her not being able to improve on nature in his case, but she still had to mask the shine on his cheeks and see that his hair was right for the part he was to play.

He gave himself over to her administrations and she thought for the hundredth time that however perfectly proportioned his face looked, it was in fact slightly lopsided, with one black eyebrow straight and the other crooked. He had a crop of very pale freckles beneath his eyes which gave him that vaguely vulnerable look beloved by the advertisers and public alike. It was plain to see that he was going to continue to be a highly paid male model for many a long day yet.

The commercials were being made for the world-wide famous firm of health food stores, J F Rabbion and Sons, and the slogan 'I'd rather have a Rabbion' had become a household phrase since Kieron had started filming them two years ago. It referred to a once-mundane muesli bar made from yogurt and honey which the nation had taken to their bosom.

Romy had worked on three adverts to date, in Russia, Brazil and India and found there was never a dull moment.

Red Square had looked beautiful covered in two feet of snow but filming had been undertaken in sub zero temperatures and the cameras had seized up. The filming had been delayed while replacements were sent and the crew had been entertained in grand style by their Russian counterparts. The landscape was breathtaking and Moscow was a beautiful city full of art galleries and palaces. And the Russians certainly knew how to throw a party. She had enjoyed herself enormously.

She hadn't enjoyed Belen in Brazil. They had arrived during an industrial dispute and there were no local porters available to carry their equipment into the jungle. They had been exhausted and dehydrated by the time they had humped the cameras and equipment over rough paths and across streams, and it was several days before they could start filming.

In Delhi the camera crew had been arrested for creating a disturbance when they had advertised for ten extras and two hundred had turned up. While matters were being sorted out the rest of them were left to their own devices. Romy had seen the Taj Mahal and been to Amritsar. It had been like a holiday, all expenses paid.

Oh no, there was never a dull moment working on the Rabbion commercials.

Romy took a huge dusting brush to Shane's shiny cheeks. "How are you getting on with the camels?" she enquired conversationally. "Decima hates them."

He gave a low chuckle "I'm not exactly enamoured with them myself," he replied with classic understatement. His accent was pure public school and so deep and vibrant it made her toes curl up in her sandals.

He pulled a disagreeable face. "One of the devils tried to bite me yesterday. If it hadn't been for Kieron pulling it off me I might not have been able to work today. As it was he got bitten instead of me. You don't know what diseases those animals are carrying."

Romy shuddered.

He leaned forward and studied his reflection. "You've missed a bit there," he said pointing to the deep cleft in his chin.

"Deliberately," she told him.

"How come?"

"Kieron told me to emphasise your . . . manliness." Romy immediately went a deep shade of pink and could not look Shane straight in the eye.

"Manliness!" he repeated with amusement. "How flattered I am to receive a compliment from you." He laughed heartily, a deep-throated sound which made her pulses tingle.

He was okay, she thought, but like all male models, incredibly vain.

"What are you doing today?" She picked up the script which was covered with her make-up fingerprints. "Oh yes, you're going through the sandstorm." She shook her head, "I don't know why I bother to get you smart and nice when you're going to end up looking like a dried prune."

The clapper-board boy put his head round the tent flap. "Mr Shelley, are you ready?"

"Just coming." He bounded out of the chair, gave Romy a quick hug and disappeared after the boy.

Romy tidied the tent and presently went outside. The heat was exhausting even so early in the morning, twenty five degrees at least. Romy guessed her sponge would be put to full use and she made sure she had a good supply of water in her portable container which she wore clipped to her belt.

She settled herself in the chair where the director could see her and prepared for another long day.

They were near the site of the three pyramids at Giza and in the distance she could see the first of the days' sightseeing coaches arriving.

The shooting of this scene involved Decima sitting on a camel. It was led by one of the Egyptian handlers. who stayed out of sight, so that she appeared to be jogging along gracefully. However the camel had other ideas. It refused to budge and Mustapha, the camel-handler, raised his arms in a helpless gesture.

"It is no good, sire, today the worthy one is not in the mood for work."

Kieron was rapidly losing patience. "That was your excuse yesterday, Mustapha. It cost me several hundred piastres for you to get him the new halter that wouldn't chafe his neck. Where is it, by the way?"

Mustapha wheedled, "He wouldn't let me put it on him."

"A likely story." Kieron mouthed in an undertone to Romy. "Their treatment of the animals is quite barbaric by our standards. I can't imagine him putting up with any nonsense." Aloud he said, "How much do you want now?"

Mustapha looked cut to the quick and the shrug he gave spoke volumes. "Sire. The worthy one needs a better diet. The food he eats . . . "

"How much?"

They eventually agreed a price and Mustapha led the camel away, promising to return within the hour.

Kieron decided to film the sandstorm sequence instead and the wind machines were sent for.

Romy made use of the break by having a cup of tea She knew she would be required to be continually on hand for the forthcoming scene and might not get another chance for refreshment.

The tea/oddjob girl, Sharon, busy with her trolley, gave an exaggerated sigh. "The extras are all a bunch of con merchants if you ask me and that Mustapha is the worse of the lot."

Romy agreed. "You may very well be right."

At last the filming got under way. Romy thought it was very exciting. The *Rabbion* Man always had to go through hell and high water to impress the *Rabbion* girl and in this particular commercial he was required to ride a camel down a steep slope into a bazaar, leap off at the bottom to wrestle with the three attackers, vanquish them and ride on through a sandstorm. He would eventually present the girl with a casket of jewels to which she would reply in the time honoured way, "I'd rather have a *Rabbion*."

It was so different from working in Alex's unit. They had been engaged on breakfast cereals with down-to-earth characters and situations. Once more her thoughts flew to him and to the day they had first met.

He had been attentive and utterly charming. And also very kind to a new girl. There was nothing too trivial that he wouldn't stop to explain to her. She had stayed behind one night to study the next day's agenda and had not known he was still in his office until he had appeared in the doorway, stretching and yawning.

"That's what I like to see, keenness," he greeted her, "But there's no need to burn the midnight oil. We don't want any wrinkles on that pretty face."

She winced at his clumsy attempt at a compliment and smiled.

"Why don't I take you out for a Chinese?" he'd offered. "There's a great little place across the road."

She opened her mouth to say 'no' but the look in his eyes sent a bolt of sheer desire down her backbone that the word came out as 'yes'. She remembered her manners and added, "Please."

By the end of the week she was in love. They had become a couple — Romy and Alex — and neither was invited to a party without the other.

Oh, why did he have to turn out so unreasonable? The day she decided she couldn't go on any more, stuck in her mind. It was a time to set her calendar by — before or after Alex.

He had laughed at first and tried to bluff it out, then he had seen she was deadly serious. He couldn't understand what was troubling her and begged her to reconsider. She was the best thing that had ever happened to him, he insisted. He didn't want to lose her. If he had done something wrong then he would try to change.

She could see it was no good. He didn't understand, would never understand. It had to be a clean break after all

The wind machines arrived and were set up. Romy was glad of her turban because the sand was disturbed over a wide area. She pulled her white smock tighter around her. Even so the sand managed to get inside her collar and, although she changed from sandals to shoes, it got between her toes. She detested the gritty feel of it.

By the time the scene was in the can, the camel had returned.

"I hope the worthy one's had a good feed," said Kieron dryly.

"Oh yes, sire, he is very satisfied."

"Well, thank goodness for that."

Romy and Sharon exchanged glances and giggled.

The shooting got under way again and Romy dodged about with the sponge dabbing first Decima's cheek then Shane's.

After about an hour they had a visitor. A golden-coloured Rolls Royce, driven by an Arab arrived and out stepped a sheik in flowing white clothes. He was tall and very dark and looked rather incongruous standing beside a little knot of ragged onlookers. Kieron asked Sharon to fetch another chair and invited their distinguished guest to sit between him and Romy.

The newcomer introduced himself as Sheik Abu Ben Talid but the name meant nothing to Romy. Kieron however had heard of him and whispered to her, "He's a great philanthropist and supports the arts. If we play our cards right we might get invited to his palace. It's just outside Cairo and I've heard it's fabulous in the true sense of the word."

The sheik took his seat and prepared to watch the proceedings, although Romy noticed he seemed to be watching her also, but not in a way that a man usually watches a woman. His interest appeared to be almost fatherly.

The camel was well-behaved now but Decima was still plainly uneasy.

"We can't film you looking scared." Kieron stood up and stroked his chin. "Even if we hide your face, your demeanor is all wrong. You're too uptight."

"Sorry, Kieron," said Decima, "it just terrifies me."

His eye fell on Romy. "Hm, you're the same height . . . "

Romy swallowed hard. "Hey, hold on a minute . . . "

"You've only got to sit on it. Please. Your face won't be seen so there's no need for make-up . . . "

She tried to think of an excuse. "But the trade union . . . "

"I'll take care of them. Well, what do you say?"

She was tongue-tied and could barely nod.

"Good girl!"

2

STANDING in for Decima meant putting on the filmy costume and Kieron announced a ten minute break while Romy and the model went to the tent to change over the garment.

"You're crazy," said Decima with a shudder. "Fancy actually agreeing to ride a camel when you don't have to. I mean there's nothing in your contract to say you have to. All the same I'm grateful to you." She paused. "Have you ever ridden a camel before?"

"No! Not even at the zoo," admitted Romy.

"Well, more fool you."

When she returned to where the cameramen were waiting patiently, she was more worried about the length of her skirt than the camel. She was no model and felt acutely embarrassed showing so much leg.

And the cameramens' whistles didn't improve the situation.

Nevertheless, she was prepared to do what was required of her and in the event it really wasn't so bad.

It was a strange feeling sitting on the beast. She seemed very high up. The camel had a swinging gait and whenever it lowered its head she felt as if she were sitting on the edge of a precipice.

The handler coaxed it along and the cameras rolled. Kieron did a thumbs up sign. It was in the can.

"Well, how does it feel being a star?" asked Shane, tongue in cheek. "Tuppence to speak to you now, I suppose."

"I won't let it change my life." Romy laughed excitedly. "Does anyone want my autograph now, while it's cheap?"

"When the commercial comes out you'll be able to point and say 'hey that's me'," Martin joined in. "Not that anyone will believe you."

Kieron patted her on the back. "Well done, my dear."

Romy had to admit she did feel good. It had been exhilarating and she was immensely satisfied with her performance.

Sheik Talid rose from his chair. "My dear young lady," he began, in a voice that sounded as if it was steeped in black molasses. "You were magnificent." He bent low over her hand and kissed it.

"Oh, er . . . " Romy was covered in confusion. Up close she could see he was quite old, as old as her father at least. "Thank you very much."

The sheik, with his dark eyes on Romy and his hand still clasping hers, announced they were all invited to his palace that evening to be entertained. "This sort of thing is good for the cementing of friendly relations between our two countries," he added.

"There goes that drink we were going to have," Martin whispered in Romy's ear as the Rolls was driven majestically away. "I can't ask you to forgo an invitation like that. Especially as the sheik plainly fancies you."

Romy felt the colour surge to her cheeks. "He was just being polite. Goodness, he's old enough to be my father."

"Well, don't say I didn't warn you." He paused dramatically. "When you end up in his harem."

She grinned. "We can have that drink tomorrow."

"I'm counting on it."

The filming continued well into the afternoon. Shane completed his camel ride and Martin stood in for him in the scene where he was attacked. In the rushes it really was impossible to detect that a stand-in had been used.

All too soon the light went and Kieron called it a day.

"Thanks everybody. I shall expect to see you at six tomorrow morning, bright-eyed and bushy-tailed, so be careful what you drink at the palace tonight."

For their evening out they were transported in a fleet of air-conditioned minibuses to an oasis some miles from their hotel. Cairo's evening rush hour was in full swing. Crowded at the best of times, this vast city with its mosques and palaces set amid the modern skyscrapers was teeming with humanity.

As the palace came into view everyone gasped out loud at its beauty. A huge single storey building, dazzlingly white, with minarets, it came straight out of the Arabian Nights.

Romy had always pictured an oasis as a small plot of green in a vast desert and she had been most surprised to learn they had several towns on them.

As they were driven into the courtyard, a giant fountain met their gaze. It was adorned with stone naiads in various stages of undress, running, leaping and flying through the air, the water cascading through shells that they held aloft. Merely looking at it made Romy feel cool.

The sheik himself met them at the vast wrought-iron doors and he was accompanied by two men holding aloft great peacock-feathered fans.

"Welcome!" the sheik boomed out and Romy had a fit of the giggles thinking he was going to add 'to my humble abode'.

Martin caught her eye and they smiled at each other and it was good to know someone else shared her sense of humour.

She smoothed the skirt of her linen suit. It was a delicate shade of crushed strawberry and she had bought it for a small fortune especially for the trip. Her silk blouse was pale grey which emphasized the gentian blueness of her eyes.

The sheik led them through several massive ornate doors to a large room where a long buffet table was laid with all manner of food. There were Western dishes as well as Arabian, Romy was relieved to note. She had heard some horrific stories about Arab hospitality and had been dreading being asked to eat sheeps' eyeballs. It was probably one of those stories that did the rounds. Like the one about the father being offered twenty camels for his daughter.

The table was flanked by an army of chefs and waiters all eager to satisfy the merest whim of the guests.

Romy couldn't help thinking that it was a bit different from her home in Brighton, and she marvelled that a child from a middle class English family could one day gaze upon a fairytale palace such as this.

A wave of homesickness swept through her unexpectedly and, before she brushed it away, she wallowed for a moment on thoughts of home. Her father was a bank manager and her mother a hospital therapist. The latter had some experience in cosmetic surgery and had been a mine of information once Romy had decided what she wanted to do. Romy's only brother, Brock, was a purser on a cruise ship, currently in the Caribbean. She corresponded with him regularly and would have a fine story to tell him this time.

Despite the intense heat outside it was deliciously cool within the palace. Romy filled a plate with various canapes and accepted a glass of red wine which Martin acquired for her from a passing tray.

She accompanied him to a silken couch and flopped down. "This is the life."

At once the sheik was by their side. To Martin he said, "Would you mind if I spirit your charming companion away for a moment?"

Martin opened and shut his mouth, at a loss for words, then he rose to his feet. Ignoring Romy's look of alarm, he murmured gallantly, "Not at all," and moved away.

Sheik Abu Ben Talid held out his hand to Romy. "Come. Do not be afraid," he whispered in her ear as if he had been reading her mind. His deep voice was compelling and seemed to hold all the mysteries of the east. She couldn't have resisted him if she had tried.

She deposited her plate and glass on a small table and allowed him to pull her from the couch.

"I expect you are wondering why I have singled you out . . . "

"Why, er no, not at all . . . "

"It is because you remind me of my late wife. She was a pure English rose too and very young." His eyes clouded for a moment. "She died in childbirth."

"Oh, I am sorry."

He tucked her hand under his arm and led her towards a low doorway which opened onto a wide corridor. "I have learned to live with my loss."

She felt a little tremor of consternation realising they were alone. Lord! What had she done, leaving the safety of the group. Abu Ben Talid might think she was his to do with as he liked.

"It was four years ago. I have learned that life goes on."

She knew instinctively that he spoke the truth and that she was safe with him.

"Do you want to talk about her?" she offered.

"What is there to say? She was my second wife," he explained. "Very young and lovely. We were married such a short time."

Romy sensed a great sadness in him.

They reached the end of the corridor and came to a labyrinth of smaller passages in which were many doors. He flung open the first to reveal a magnificent library. The room was filled with the rich smell of hundreds of leather-tooled, gold-lettered books, and the unstained sycamore shelves glinted like satin in the rays of the setting sun pouring in the tall windows.

Romy went forward with a gasp of delight. "Oh! I love books. Just the feel of them . . . Have you any English volumes?"

"My dear young lady." Abu Ben

Talid threw back his head and laughed in that throaty way of his. "I have first editions of most of your Charles Dickens' novels. I have the complete works of Shakespeare. I have Chaucer in the original old English Gothic text." He paused for breath. "And that's not all. I even have Just William and Enid Blyton's Famous Five."

"That's put me in my place." She grinned.

"Come!" he beckoned again. "I want you to see the desert in all it's all glory."

"Oh yes?" she gulped.

"It's good having the film crew here," he said as he led her into the wide corridor again, "It gives us a chance to exchange cultural ideas."

He drew her onto a flower-decked terrace and slid his arm around her as with his free hand he pointed away over the low wall to the desert beyond. "Isn't it marvellous?"

She was so nervous, she answered

flippantly. "It looks like a lot of sand to me."

"Oh no, you are quite wrong." His arm tightened about her waist. "It is a place that can make or break a man. And a woman too, I think."

She sensed he was passing on some ancient folklore and kept quiet so as not to break the spell.

"There are no illusions out there," he continued, "only the truth. The desert shrinks you to a tiny dot and yet the very dwarfing exalts the soul. It is easy to understand why the prophets of old and the wise men took refuge in a desert, for elsewhere their ideas would have seemed absurd."

Silently she watched the animated expressions crossing his dark features and was suddenly breathless for him to go on, to tell her more of this land which he regarded so sublimely.

"Imagination has room to grow in the desert," he said proudly. "All my ideas of life are forced into perspective when I look across those dunes and hear the sighing of the wind. Believe me, Romy, after you have seen the desert, really seen it, you are never the same again. Its vistas tell you things you would not otherwise dream of. It terrifies and comforts at one and the same time. It is a vacuum devoid of human beings and so it feeds the mind. It lies in wait, beckoning like a sensuous woman. What man could resist it?" He blinked suddenly and laughed self-consciously. "I must sound ridiculous!"

"No, I'm fascinated," she contradicted him. He was a strange man, she thought, not at all as she expected.

There was a movement behind them and Romy turned to see a little girl, no more than three or four, pressing herself back against the wall as if she wanted to be invisible. Her skin was dark and her long hair was jet black but the most arresting feature about her was her eyes — huge and dark and shining like jewels. She wore a silk tunic in an exotic shade of pink and there were gold slippers on her tiny feet.

"Tanita!" The sheik bent and scooped her into his arms. He spoke softly to her in his own tongue and she answered hesitantly.

"This," he said addressing Romy, "is my daughter, Tanita, my pride and joy, my most precious gem."

Romy smiled and held out her hand. "I'm pleased to meet you, Tanita."

The child turned her head and buried her face in her father's shoulder.

Abu Ben Talid smiled. "She is shy, but she wanted to see my guests so gave her nurse the slip, dressed herself and came to join the party."

He took a deep steadying breath. "As you can see, Tanita is the reason for my life. I live in fear of kidnappers. Last year we had a scare when Tanita was missing for an hour." He forced a smile. "But enough about such frightening things on this fine evening."

At that moment a distraught-looking woman dressed in a long flowing black robe came along the terrace uttering a terrible wailing noise. At the sight of Tanita in her father's arms she clasped her hands together and seemed to be saying a prayer. Abu Ben Talid handed the child over to the woman, who was obviously her nurse, and the two of them departed.

"What a beautiful child!" exclaimed Romy.

"Yes, I think so."

"Is she your only child?"

"No, I have two sons by a previous marriage. They are both fully grown and married. Alas their mother also is dead."

Tucking her arm through his, he drew her from the terrace. Back in the main hall he released her into Martin's safe-keeping once more.

"Thank you so much for showing me your desert," she said. "And I count myself privileged to have met Tanita."

"It was a pleasure, my dear." He clapped his hands in a dramatic way.

This seemed to be a signal for a small troupe of musicians to enter and begin to play their stringed instruments. They were joined by two belly dancers, one young and slender, the other of ample proportions.

Kieron came to sit beside them on the couch. "Enjoying yourself, Romy?"

She nodded. "Hm! The sheik's an interesting fellow." She was prepared to tell him all the sheik had said but she suddenly realised the director seemed pale, which was unusual for him. With his boyish features he always appeared the picture of health. "Are you feeling all right?" she asked tentatively.

He shivered. "Am I imagining it or is it very cold in here?"

"It's cool, thanks to the fans, but not excessively so."

He wiped his hand across his brow. "Now it feels hot," he said, tearing at his collar. "What's happening to me?"

"Kieron!" There was a note of alarm in her voice as she remembered the camel bite he had sustained. "Did you get that bite looked at?"

"No, it hardly seemed worth it." He pushed up his sleeve and they both gasped at the ugly raw wound, the centre of which could actually be seen to be throbbing.

"Oh, my God!" exclaimed Romy.

"Hell! I didn't know it looked like that. It's been aching slightly all day but it was okay when I checked it earlier this evening."

He stood up and Romy jumped up after him. She saw him sway about and called out to Martin, "Quickly, catch him! He's going to faint!"

Martin moved with the speed of light and caught the director just in time to prevent him from hitting the floor.

He laid him gently on the couch. Romy thought at the back of her mind that with all his strength Martin could also be incredibly tender.

Abu Ben Talid ordered Kieron to be taken to a side room. Martin picked him up again and bore him easily to the room the sheik indicated, accompanied by Romy. When the others tried to follow the sheik shut the door in their faces.

"Too many people are bad for him," he explained.

There was a couch in the corner of the room and Kieron was deposited on it.

Romy stared at Martin. "What shall we do?" she cried with mounting hysteria.

The sheik took command of the situation. "Leave everything to me," he said in a calming voice. "My personal physician is in residence and has been sent for."

As he spoke the door opened and in walked a tall distinguished-looking man in Western dress, carrying a small black briefcase.

"Ah, doctor!" the sheik greeted him. "Thank you for coming so promptly."

He looked grave as he asked Romy and Martin a few questions. Then he shooed them out of the room while he made his examination.

Romy realized she was holding her breath. The crew strode about looking anxious. When the door opened some fifteen minutes later they crowded around it.

The doctor held up a hand for quiet. "He is very weak and must be operated on at once or risk losing his arm."

Sharon, the general dogsbody, burst into tears.

Martin put an arm around her trembling shoulders. "It's all right, love. He'll get the best possible treatment."

"Are you taking him to hospital, doctor?" asked Romy.

The sheik answered her. "We have our very own hospital here," he said with justifiable pride, "with all the latest equipment. The best that money can buy."

The doctor said, "Your director is not conscious and cannot give his permission for me to operate, so I will take it as a matter of life and death and go ahead. Has anyone any objections?"

There was a murmur of conversation but no-one objected.

Kieron was placed on a trolley and taken away along the corridor.

The crew watched till he was out of sight. A feeling of doom had descended on the gathering and no-one felt inclined to carry on with the party.

One by one they drifted outside and were ferried back to their hotel. As Romy got ready for bed, her mind reeled with worries about Kieron's health and the likelihood of his being able to continue with the filming. This project seemed to be jinxed, more so than the others, what with the unco-operativeness of the camel-handlers and now this. Would the commercial ever be finished?

She got out her writing set and penned a letter to her brother. She told Brock all about the camel ride and how good she felt about it. 'Perhaps I missed my calling,' she wrote knowing full well she wouldn't change jobs with Decima for the world.

She picked up her hairbrush and went to the window to gaze out over the city, recalling what the sheik had said. She thought she might like to take a trip into the desert now that he had whetted her appetite.

* * *

"Kieron's been operated on," Martin informed the crew the following morning when they assembled in the hotel foyer. "It was touch and go for a while but the doctor is confident he'll pull through. The next twenty-four hours will be crucial."

Shane Shelley ambled into view. "The head cameraman has sent for another director," he said. "He should be arriving about now."

As he spoke a limousine drew up outside. Romy glanced idly towards the car door as the replacement director stepped out.

Suddenly she froze. She had an awful premonition before she actually saw his face. Something about the confident way he held himself, the buoyant way he walked . . .

She felt the hairs on the back of her neck begin to tingle. Then it was as if she had turned to stone.

"Oh no!" she murmured. "Not Alex . . . "

As he walked towards her it was as if time stood still. She had idly daydreamed about how she would behave if she came face to face with him again. Sometimes she fancied she would cut him dead. It would be good to see him humiliated and unsure of himself. Sometimes a clever remark would suffice, something icily courteous or devastatingly contemptuous. But now the moment was here and she could do nothing but gape at him.

He was marvellously tanned and his blond hair was bleached almost white by the sun. She was to find out later he'd been recalled from leave to stand in for Kieron and flown here directly from Singapore.

"Hi, Romy," he greeted her casually enough, but she detected a note of bitterness in his voice.

"Hi!" she rejoined, bringing all her reserves of composure into play.

Her gaze took in his crumpled linen suit and the twenty-four-hour growth of stubble on his chin. He looked vulnerable somehow and she felt herself being drawn to him against her will

He turned to speak with Shane and she escaped outside into the hotel garden. Here was a cool haven under the tall palms and a majestic fountain played in the centre. She took several deep breaths before she was even able to think properly.

She was trembling from head to foot like an autumn leaf caught in a gale. She must pull herself together soon or she would be no good at her job. A steady hand was needed with make-up or you could do someone an injury — poke their eye out or give them a nasty jab with a hot hair wand.

As she stood by the fountain she heard the crunch of shoes on gravel and turned to see Shane.

"What's the matter, Romy, my dear?" he drawled. "You look like you've seen a ghost."

She mulled over his remark. A ghost? Of her past? "Perhaps I have," she replied slowly. "Yes. A ghost."

"Now don't you go all sloppy on me." He took her elbow. "Come on, you'll be late on the set." And he escorted back to the foyer where the others were preparing to leave.

The crew made their way to the desert location and Romy set about getting her tent ready. She had just finished when Decima came in.

"Say, are you all right?" she asked. "You looked ghastly when Alex arrived." She peered into Romy's face. "And you don't look too good now." Shrewdly, she added, "It's almost as if you two have been very close and fallen out."

Romy couldn't hide the telltale blush that rose so readily to her cheeks.

Decima let out a low whistle. "So it's true. You're the girl they were talking about back home. The one who's rumoured to be responsible for Alex's recent black moods."

Romy opened her mouth to say she didn't know anything about black moods but Decima hadn't finished.

"Oh yes. My room-mate is in his team and she says lately he's the devil to work for."

Romy gulped.

"So you're the girl. I would never have guessed. He's always been a bit of a lad apparently. But lately they'd noticed he'd calmed down. He appeared to be growing up at last. That was your influence, I suppose. Well, let's face it. You're a quiet one. I mean you're not exactly the life and soul of the party."

She looked at Romy with enquiring eyes. "I always wondered what sort of girl could tame Alex Kruger. I didn't think it would be a little nobody like you."

Romy gasped at the insensitivity of the remark.

Decima gave an apologetic little cough. "Oh, I'm sorry, Romy. That was an unkind thing to say." She glanced away. "What I meant to say was, we all thought it was someone famous because he works with glamorous actresses and models all day and can have his pick of them." She leaned forward and studied her reflection in the mirror. "Still, I suppose he gets sick of seeing beautiful bodies all his working days and prefers to see someone a bit plainer in his free time."

Romy said nothing although the apology had only made the insult worse. It was no good having a shouting match with Decima. The model was stunning to look at but completely dim, being interested only in things that concerned herself. She really believed she had put matters right and to argue would have been a waste of Romy's breath.

Alex came into the tent. He had changed into shorts and a cheesecloth shirt and looked relaxed and cool, though she realised he must be suffering from jet-lag. He actually seemed embarrassed. "Romy, I want you to emphasize Decima's eyes even more. Can you add some gold to the silver on her lids."

"But Kieron already tried that . . ." began Romy.

"No doubt," he said tersely. "But I'm running the show now."

"Yes, I'm sorry."

He stood looking at her for long moments his head on one side. Then he turned on his heel and ducked out under the flap.

"Ooh!" said Decima, "He doesn't like you one little bit."

Romy forced a shrug. "So what? That's his problem."

"Could be yours too," warned the model. "If he chooses to make something of it. It's not wise to fall out with the director. He could make things difficult for you, even send you off the set."

She half-turned round in the chair and stared at Romy. "Oh, don't fall out with him, please. I'd hate to lose you. You're the best make up artist I've ever had."

"Well, thanks for that vote of confidence," said Romy tightlipped. "Don't worry. Alex knows I'm good." She took a pad of cotton wool soaked in baby oil and proceeded to build up the eye colour. "He's a professional if nothing else. He won't let personal feelings get in the way of progress."

Decima again peered hard into the mirror to see the effect of the gold shadow. She sighed. "It's not going to work, is it?"

"No, Kieron abandoned the idea because your skin is too fair."

"Are you going to tell him or am I?" joked Decima.

"Oh, let Mr Clever Clogs find out for himself."

After she had finished the model girl's makeup, Romy went outside to see if filming was ready to start.

"We're doing the bazaar scene on

location." Alex informed them. "We'll go there straight away by minibus."

The rest of the crew, there were sixteen of them altogether, were already aboard. Alex said, "Be careful not to mess up your face, Decima. I shall want you in close-up first thing." He hooked a finger under Decima's chin and studied her critically. Over his shoulder he said, "You've done a good job, Romy, exactly as I wanted it."

"Thank you." Her tone was clipped as she thought that it was all wasted because Decima's skin wouldn't take such deep colours.

But she was proved wrong. The bazaar was an eerie place full of dark and light patches and for some reason deeper shades were necessary. In fact Romy wished now that she had darkened Shane's eyelids too.

"How did you know it would work?" she asked Alex later when they stopped for coffee.

"I've filmed in a similar bazaar before," he admitted, taking a mug from Sharon's trolley. "I don't know what it is but the light is uncanny." He leaned towards her and lowered his voice. "Romy, we must talk."

She watched him in alarm. "Oh no. I've said all I have to say."

"Oh, Romy."

She stood up and began to move away. "No, Alex, I mean it."

"I thought that now the dust has had time to settle . . . "

"No, Alex."

He gripped her arm, his fingers digging in like steel clamps making her tremble all over. He brought his mouth close to her ear. "I still want to marry you, Romy," he whispered urgently.

She tugged her arm away. "Don't!"

No-one would ever know how much it cost her in heartache and frayed nerves to walk briskly away and back to the makeup tent which had been brought with the other equipment on the lorry. She felt drained of emotions as she washed the table. He didn't know how near he had come to breaking down all her defences.

Nor must he know. That chapter of her life was over. She had dared to play the game of love and it hadn't worked out. The fire had been so intense she had got her fingers badly burned. There was no way she was going to risk it again. And yet . . . she had thrilled to his touch just then. The pressure of his fingers seemed to have branded her though she could see no mark. She had throbbed with desire from his declaration that he still wanted to marry her. She must conduct herself very carefully if she didn't want to precipitate a disaster.

Inside the tent she peeped out through one of the smeary plastic windows and watched him. He was scowling

Involuntarily she shivered.

In the afternoon they travelled to the sheik's oasis again. He had agreed to let them use it for the next scene. There was a leafy haven behind the palace with water from a spring flowing through it.

Directly they arrived the sheik came out to join them.

"Your colleague is responding to the post-operative treatment," he informed them. "He is allowed visitors now so you could go and see him this evening after filming."

"Oh good!" said Romy, "I'll buy him some grapes."

While Alex was getting the set ready, Romy helped to break open a fresh box of *Rabbion*. The product had suffered somewhat from the heat and the delay and looked decidedly limp.

Shane took a bar in his hand. "I don't think she would prefer a *Rabbion* if this is what it looks like." He bit the end off and pulled a face. "Ugh!" He spat it out. "It's horrible. It's gone off."

"You shouldn't have bitten into it," Romy scolded. "You don't know what the high temperature is doing to the ingredients. You could find yourself a casualty like Kieron."

He watched her from half closed eyes. "And that would worry you, would it?" His voice vibrated, low and husky. "You'd be worried if little old me got laid up?"

She shot him a look of censure, her eyes flashing blue fire. "Of course I would worry. With you laid up the filming would never be finished. The thought of remaining in this God-forsaken place one day more than necessary fills me with dread." She reflected that until this morning she had quite liked the desert, but the arrival of Alex has spoilt everything.

Shane turned down the corners of his mouth. "And there I was thinking you were concerned for me. I dared to think there might be a chance for me. But no. You certainly know how to hurt a guy." His hand shot out to cup her chin and he forced her to look at him. "Would it be so terrible if you fancied me one little bit?"

She clerked her chin from his grasp

and laughed wryly. “You and your ego! No it wouldn’t be so terrible. It would be impossible.” She swung away from him and his chuckle reverberated in her ears. Shane she could handle.

3

AS soon as Alex saw the state of the product he ordered a new supply to be flown out from London. Meanwhile the damaged goods could be used for the rehearsals.

But no sooner had they arranged them for the close-up photographs, when several desert dogs came sniffing around and the place was soon swarming with flies.

"I just don't need all this aggravation," muttered Alex.

Romy took refuge in her tent and she was surprised when Alex joined her.

"Look Romy, we can't go on like this, not speaking about the break-up of our engagement." He perched on the edge of the dressing table, swinging one long leg. "I hoped you'd have had time to get over this nonsense. Saying I was possessive indeed!" He scratched at the stubble on his chin. "If I was possessive it was because I love you!"

"Please Alex we've been through all this."

He reached out and took her wrist. "You must give me a second chance."

Trembling, she shook him away. "There's no must about it."

For long moments he gazed at her. "Romy?"

"No, no, I can't . . . "

With relief she saw Decima come into the tent.

"Ow! Those flies are all in my hair. They got right under the wig . . . " She saw Alex and stopped. "Oh, I'm sorry. I'll go out again."

Alex rose from the table. "It's all right. I'm going." With a glance at Romy that indicated he hadn't finished with her, he ducked out of the tent.

Decima dropped into the chair and tossed the wig down. "I hope I didn't interrupt anything." She carefully touched her red hair, separating the strands and peering anxiously into the mirror. "If it's not one thing it's another."

"I suppose the flies are attracted to the hairspray on the wig," observed Romy.

She was shaking uncontrollably. Any more physical contact with Alex and she would be a nervous wreck. Why didn't he leave her alone? Did he really still want her or was he just taking advantage of the situation. Because she was there.

She tackled the problem of Decima's hair, ridding her of the flies. When she reset the wig, she disposed with the spray and used water instead As she finished the clapper-board boy was at the tent flap with word that rehearsals were about to start.

This scene involved a kiss to be bestowed on Decima by Shane, a full-blooded kiss delivered squarely on the mouth. They had to have several tries before they got it to Alex's satisfaction. Romy, on call with the lipbrush, had to keep dashing forward and she felt like a gooseberry spoiling the clinches. She thought that Shane appeared to be enjoying the experience. He just didn't seem to be acting. But then he made no secret of the fact that he liked women.

The rest of the day, spent back at the original set, passed smoothly enough, if you didn't count the heat and the short tempers that it generated. Romy was relieved when Alex announced they would finish and start again extra early in the morning.

"This oasis is a little bit of cool heaven in an otherwise unfriendly environment," remarked Alex "I wouldn't like to live in the desert. It's far too arid."

Romy had an image of the sheik and the glow in his eyes as he had told her about his love of it and tried to put the other side of the story. "Oh, I don't know. Sheik Abu Ben Talid thinks it strengthens a man's character. He almost convinced me it was paradise." She saw Alex looking at her in a puzzled fashion and stopped, feeling self-conscious.

"Well," he declared, "I'm glad I'm only standing in for Kieron and that he's on the mend."

That evening Romy and Martin went into the palace to see Kieron. They found him sitting up in bed reading the script.

"Does the doctor know you're doing that?" scolded Romy, placing a bag of grapes on the bedside table and bending over to kiss his cheek.

He grinned sheepishly.

He told them he would be confined to bed for the best part of a week and Romy's heart sank. There was no getting out of it. Alex was here to stay.

* * *

It seemed to have become normal practice to go to the palace every night.

"I find watching the filming quite fascinating," said the sheik to Romy and Sharon, as they strolled through the courtyard, "but I understand all your efforts to date will amount to two minutes screen time. Can that be possible?"

"That's right," Romy replied.

"It's amazing."

He had again put on some entertainment and fifty men, burnous-clad, rode their horses into the courtyard where a black tent had been erected. Several women dressed in traditional white robes came to kneel outside the tent entrance while the men proceeded to drill their mounts in an impressive display of close harmony riding.

Romy was enthralled. She had forgotten her argument with Alex and was feeling relaxed and thankful for the cool breeze that wafted in from the desert.

Shane was lolling beside her on one of the canvas chairs which had been brought out to make them comfortable.

"Tell me, is it true?" he drawled lazily. "There's a rumour going round that you and the director were engaged at one time."

"Mind your own business!"

"It explains everything," he continued unabashed. "Why you're so jumpy and argumentative."

"I am not argumentative!" she snapped.

A slow smile spread over his handsome face. "I rest my case."

He was so easy-going, she couldn't stay mad at him and she granted him a little smile.

"That's better," he said. "You don't want to fight everyone. I'm on your side."

Seeing Alex bearing down on her, she jumped up and made an elaborate search in her bag for a handkerchief.

"Romy . . ."

"I'm sorry, Alex, I'm going back to the hotel as soon as this display is over. I'm absolutely bushed. I've got to get my head down or I'll be no good tomorrow."

"Very well." He turned curtly away.

Almost immediately she felt a hand on her shoulder and looked up to see Martin towering above her.

"How about that drink when we leave here?"

Romy felt she must refuse because of what she'd told Alex. She feigned a yawn. "I'm sorry, Martin. As I've just told Alex, it's been an awful day. I'm tired and sticky. All I want to do after this is finished is get back to the hotel, have a shower and get my head down."

His face fell.

She felt mean. "Oh, all right. I'm sorry, Martin, I didn't intend to sound irritable." She grinned. "A long cool lager will go down a treat."

"Good." He had changed into a pair of 501 jeans and a classic white teeshirt which emphasised his muscular build, making him appear magnificently virile.

As soon as the horse-riding display came to an end Romy and Martin left the palace.

Shane's gaze followed them, a strange

brooding gaze, thought Romy. Why, he almost looked jealous before he gave a little shrug and turned away. She decided she must have imagined it, probably a trick of the light, and tucked her arm under Martin's.

He led her to the minibus which acted as a kind of shuttle between the palace and their Cairo hotel

The heat of the day was tempered by a cool breeze now and Romy's hair streamed out behind her as she sat by the open window. In fact it streamed all over Martin's face and she laughed as she apologised.

"Don't be sorry." He grabbed a handful of the fragrant tresses. "It feels wonderfully soft."

Their eyes met and she saw him blush suddenly. She hid a smile, conscious she had a sensitive man beside her and not wanting to frighten him off.

They arrived at the hotel and went directly to the Sheba bar. It was small and intimate with a huge fan in the ceiling, creating a most delightful breeze.

The lights were turned down low and Romy stumbled her way to a table in the corner while Martin waved to attract the waiter's attention. He joined her and they ordered their lagers.

"Hm! This is very nice," murmured Romy sipping from the ice-cold glass.

"Alone with you at last," said Martin, quickly lowering his gaze.

Romy thought that here was some progress, considering how shy he was. "Yes, we don't see much of each other on the set."

They were sitting on some kind of bench and he moved to sit beside her. "Romy . . . Romy? That's an unusual name. What does it mean?"

"I don't know. I think my mother made it up. I was conceived on a holiday in Rome. What does Martin mean?"

"Warlike, from the god Mars."

"That's a misnomer. You're not at all warlike. You're very gentle."

“Women don’t want gentle men. They prefer smoothies like Shane Shelley.”

“Don’t you believe it,” said Romy. “I certainly don’t prefer smoothies.”

His hand covered hers as it lay on the bench between them and she could feel him gradually grow calm and relaxed.

They had another half a larger each and sat for a while without speaking, but it wasn’t a strained silence. Romy had not felt this good about a man for a long time.

Martin suggested they take a walk the following evening through downtown Cairo to look at the shops.

Romy agreed and then, yawning, she left him and went to bed.

* * *

The following evening Martin reminded Romy of her promise and they took a bus to the Maydan al-Tahrir alighting in Liberation Square.

They strolled hand in hand under the

trees. The streets were crowded even at this late hour and there was an air of carnival about the place.

They came to an all night market, a labyrinth of little lanes with stalls selling every kind of merchandise — gaily-coloured materials, exotic fruits and vegetables, records, books, small pieces of furniture, and so on. Martin paused at a stall selling secondhand jewellery and delved among the pieces on the table. He plucked out a necklace of wrought silver with a jade pendant. After haggling over the price for a while, he finally paid the stall-holder what Romy considered a lot of money.

"For your girl-friend?" She teased.

"For you," he said turning to her

"Oh, thank you. It's beautiful, but you shouldn't have. Will you put it on for me?"

As he fastened it around her neck his hands shook and he was all thumbs.

"I want to buy you something," said Romy.

"Oh no . . . " he began but she was

already examining the stall. She found a little silver knife used for cutting tobacco. Although he was not a smoker she guessed he would appreciate this antique item. The look on his face as she presented it to him proved her right.

They returned to the hotel and Romy fell asleep in the chair in the lounge

"Come on sleepy head," said Martin and he escorted her to her door.

As she undressed she smiled to herself. Martin was becoming less tongue-tied by the minute. With a dreamy look on her face, she fingered the necklace. "He's nice," she said aloud. "The nicest man on the set."

* * *

The following day they were ready to shoot but the fresh case of *Rabbion* had still not arrived.

"I don't believe this!" Alex stormed about the foyer. "Look, folks, we're going to have to postpone the shooting.

I suggest you spend your free day sightseeing or washing your smalls or whatever turns you on. Me? I'm going to take Romy riding." He stared at her as if daring her to refuse him.

It was too hot to argue. With a deep sigh she gave in. "Very well."

Besides she couldn't keep dodging him. She might as well listen to what he had to say. She fetched her sunhat from her room and grabbed a lightweight jacket from the peg.

He took her in a taxi to the Salah Salem Avenue stables in the southern part of the city where he arranged the hire of two horses.

Romy enjoyed riding even though she was a novice, having only ridden the hacks at a Brighton riding school close to where she lived. She had purposely asked for a quiet horse and had been given a white-maned chestnut gelding. A young Arab boy held its head while she mounted and she noted it looked docile enough.

Alex, in contrast, who was an expert,

sat easily in the saddle of a powerful black stallion. He was all in black jeans, teeshirt, sombrero and boots, and even wore a black bandana knotted loosely about his throat. To Romy he looked devilishly attractive.

As they left the yard he said, so softly that she could only just hear, "So you were too tired to let me buy you a drink last evening. Yet you weren't too tired for Martin."

She ignored him. That was how he used to speak to her when they were engaged. He had no right then — and even less now. She was already regretting she had agreed to accompany him.

However it was pleasant enough jogging along under the brilliant blue canopy of the sky. They passed through the outskirts of Cairo till they reached the edge of the desert.

Presently Alex reined in his horse near a little clump of palm trees beside a short row of tumbledown houses which formed a kind of barrier between city and desert, and suggested they stop for a breather. As she started to dismount she mentally braced herself for a conversation she did not want and had not instigated.

Before she touched the ground his hands came up to grab her waist. She leaned on his sinewy forearms and he set her down in front of him. His hands were resting on her silky shirt warming her skin in an evocative and all too familiar way.

She laughed awkwardly and made a little movement to draw away from him, but his hands retained their hold on her and his eyes, when she dared to look at them, were frankly seductive, half-closed, smouldering.

He moved his hand to touch her hair, slowly and meticulously sifting it through his fingers, allowing the honey-bright tresses to swing about her slim shoulders in a shimmering cloud.

"You are so lovely," he whispered huskily. His hands had slipped inside her jacket and his breathing became quick and shallow.

She groaned with unexpected pleasure. Seeing him moisten his lips, a softening weakness crept through her bloodstream, veiling her mind in a languid haze. She knew he was about to kiss her and was impatient for it to happen. Leaning towards him, her body soft and yielding, she was filled with a mighty tide of emotion.

Her arms stole up to wind about his neck. Slowly his lips moved in the direction of her own. It was a tantalising moment. Then warning bells rang in her brain as sanity flooded back to her. Heavens! What was she doing? Giving Alex every reason to think she was eager to get back on the old footing.

"Stop it! Let me go!" Panic constricted her throat.

He ignored her pleas and his fingers found the zip of her blouse.

"No, no!" she cried pushing him forcefully from her.

"Don't fight your emotions," he

murmured indistinctly, "You can't live without me!"

"Oh yes I can!"

Romy stumbled blindly towards the chestnut horse startling it so that it shied away from her. She grabbed its main and scrambled into the saddle, her foot feeling desperately for the farther stirrup.

Alex shouted, "Come back, Romy, don't behave like a silly little fool!"

She looked frantically about her for a hiding place and espied a narrow alleyway just a few yards past the row of houses. As Alex ran towards his horse and mounted it, he had his back to her. She grabbed the opportunity to escape. She dug her heels in and the little horse dashed into the alleyway. She tugged on the reins and waited in the shadows till she saw Alex go by.

Then she took the opposite direction.

She was aware that her steed was still unnerved and clicked her tongue in an effort to calm it. They had travelled scarcely a hundred yards when it was startled again by a snakelike creature about three feet long travelling at speed in front of them. The mare let out a frightened whinny and raced on at an alarming rate, hurling itself forward as if all the hounds of hell were after it. They were soon out of sight of the buildings and Romy reckoned they must have gone half a mile when she noticed a large group of lizards basking in the sun directly ahead of them. Mindful of how the horse had shied at the snake, she pulled hard at the reins. It made no difference. The animal reared again and veered off the track to race across the sandy terrain.

She was partially dislodged and clung to the pommel as they sped over the uneven ground. Their flight seemed endless and as the horse made a sudden turn she was toppled from her precarious position and slid backwards. She landed in a crumpled heap on the ground, her leg captured awkwardly beneath her. The very act of scrambling to her feet brought a cry of pain from her lips. When she tried to put her weight on her right foot the pain became unbearable She hastily checked there were no bones broken but every part of her body ached.

The horse, she saw, was a little way off seeking shelter from the sun beside a thorny bush, its eyes wild, its nostrils flaring, its coat frothing with foam.

Her mouth was dry and she hobbled towards it for the flask of the life-saving water in the saddle bag but every time she managed to get near the crazed animal tossed its mane and ran a few yards further away.

The heat was intense, the sun at its zenith and she had no hat. That had got lost during the headlong dash.

She had the sense to know she must stay where she was and crawled into the semi-shade of one of the stunted thorn bushes.

How long would it be before Alex found her — or even realised she was in the desert? Her route had been tortuous and she could be anywhere. And all because he had tried to kiss her. Anything, even his kiss she reflected, would be better than dying of thirst in the desert.

As she stared at the relentless expanse of sand she detected a slight breeze which shifted the fine particles. She shivered involuntarily. Was it the start of a sand storm? She knew they blew up quite suddenly. Perhaps she was being too pessimistic.

But after a few minutes her worst fears were realised as the sand began to whip about her in a violent manner.

"Oh God!" she murmured. "What a horrible way to die!"

She must have dozed off but slept fitfully. She was disturbed by the sound of approaching horsemen. Raising her head and shielding her eyes, she observed Shane Shelley. Dressed in a voluminous burnous, an anxious look on his face, he was tethering his horse to a stunted tree.

He hurried towards her, his eyes

kind above the scarf he wore over the lower half of his face. Kneeling beside her he said, "There you are! Well, thank goodness for that. I don't particularly like riding through sandstorms."

He lifted her head a little and guided her mouth so she could sip from a goatskin bag he carried.

She eagerly gulped the life-preserving water until he said, "That's enough for the moment."

"Oh please . . . "

"No!" he said firmly. "You're too dehydrated." He applied lip-salve to her mouth. She winced despite his gentleness. She hadn't realised how cracked was her skin.

"How long have I been here?" she moaned.

"It must be an hour."

"Oh it seems so much longer."

She felt him tremble as he swung her into his arms and took a few paces towards his horse. As he moved several other horsemen rode up and dismounted. Romy recognised most of the film crew plus a few of the Arab extras. Sheik Abu Ben Talid was also there. And Alex.

Alex was the first to speak. "Romy! Forgive me!" He hastened forward and tried to take her from Shane's arms, but the male model hung on. "I've been out of my mind with worry."

Shane ignored him and lifted Romy onto his mount.

"Say something, for heaven's sake," pleaded Alex. "At least say you forgive me."

"Leave the poor girl alone," said Shane climbing into the saddle behind her.

The journey back to the hotel was hellish. Romy was bruised and aching all over and every little undulation in the landscape registered with her.

They eventually arrived and she thanked Shane for rescuing her.

"Don't thank me," he said gruffly. "The sheik organised the search party. I just went along for the ride."

She didn't believe that for a moment but let it pass.

After a good soak in the bath, Romy felt none the worse for her ordeal. She went down to the foyer only to find Alex was waiting for her. And she could see Shane hovering in the background behind a pillar that separated them from the bar.

"Romy!" Alex took her hands and pushed her gently into an armchair. "How can I make it up to you?"

"Just leave me alone, Alex," she said wearily. "I don't want you to try and make it up to me. I just want to be left alone."

Alex placed his hands on her shoulders. "Give me a break, Romy. You know we were meant for each other. Why do you persist in denying it?"

"I said leave me alone," she cried wriggling to be free of his hands. "Stop pawing me."

He dug his fingers into her flesh. "Stop being such a little fool! You. . . "

"Are you all right, Romy?" Shane had ambled over to where they were arguing. "You should be taking it easy after your ordeal."

She was grateful for his intervention but couldn't expect him to go against Alex who was the director after all.

"I'm giving everybody the day off again tomorrow," announced Alex. "The money for the extras has gone missing now and they are on strike, so it's pointless carrying on filming." He looked at Romy. "My dear, I would like to take you to the seaside resort of Helwan. There is a coach trip . . . "

"Oh but I've already promised to go with Shane." She didn't know why she had said that. She meant to have said Martin.

Shane said quickly, "That's right." He smiled. "I've already booked the tickets on the coach."

The expression that overcame Alex's face was terrible to see. He looked as if he would like to kill Shane. "There's nothing more to be said then." And with that he swivelled on his heel and marched out of the foyer.

"Oh Shane, thank you for coming over and getting me out of that awkward situation," said Romy, placing her hand on his forearm. "You don't have to take me to the seaside. I'll just hide somewhere."

"Nonsense!" he replied with a grin. "I'll nip down and get the tickets straight away." He laid one finger alongside his nose and winked. "Mum's the word."

"Are you sure?"

"Sure I'm sure."

"I've caused a lot of trouble, haven't I?" she murmured. "Having the filming postponed while everyone searched for me."

"It was a welcome diversion," said Shane. "The filming is getting most of us down. Besides it wasn't your fault. I'll wager it was Alex's."

"But everyone will blame me because they don't know the circumstances."

"And what are the circumstances? If

you don't mind my asking."

"Oh, Alex was being a pest. You were right when you thought we were once engaged. The trouble with Alex is he won't let go."

"I see," said Shane thoughtfully. "Well, don't you worry. Tomorrow you'll spend an Alex-free day."

She wished it could also be a Shane-free day but reckoned she owed him something.

* * *

"I'm looking forward to this," said Romy as she and Shane took their seats in the coach. It was a long modern vehicle and the passengers were mostly British and Americans with a handful of Egyptians. Romy and Shane had seats in the middle.

The guide warned them it would be a long ride and they sang most of the way. They journeyed for about three hours on an asphalt road travelling through villages and between palm trees.

Presently they came to the open desert where the spa town of Helwan nestled beside the Nile.

The coach driver dropped them by the southern terminus of the metro system with a reminder to those who were not going to accompany the guide to be back at four.

Romy looked about her. "I see there are lots of beautiful old houses."

"This used to be a fashionable resort," said the guide. "It's a pity they are in such a bad state of repair."

"Isn't this better than grubbing about on some old film set?" said Shane. "We've got Alex to thank for this. If he hadn't offered to bring you here you wouldn't have thought of involving me."

"To be honest I meant to say Martin was taking me," confessed Romy. "I don't know what made me say Shane."

"It was a Freudian slip." He grinned. "You really wanted to come with me but you wouldn't admit it."

She thought for the hundredth time

how vain he was but she guessed it was an occupational hazard for a male model especially one as handsome as he.

"Sure," she said flippantly. "I've fallen under your spell like all the other girls."

"Don't knock it. You might find you're speaking the truth. You don't want to mess about with old Martin. He's so dull. He makes the railway timetable read like the Booker winner."

"Oh that's not fair. Martin's very sweet."

"At least," said Shane, "he supports Watford United, so he can't be all bad."

"I also support Watford United — because my father was born there."

He squeezed her hand. "There now, I knew we'd find we had something in common if we dug deep enough."

They smiled at each other.

They descended the steps of the coach and followed the guide along a short path which led them to a Japanese garden filled with exotic blooms. The man pointed out a stream that flowed through and washed the lower stones of an arched grotto.

A little way further along he invited them to remove their shoes and they followed him into a high-domed mosque. Romy had never been in a mosque before and she was duly awed. She studied the colourful tiles on the walls. They formed patterns and she supposed they were symbolic. She whispered to Shane, "I know nothing about the Islamic faith." She glanced at a line of men on their knees facing the wall. "But they seem very devout. Should we intrude like this?"

The guide overheard her and said it was perfectly all right but Romy till felt uneasy.

"I'll wait outside," she said.

Shane accompanied her. "You have a sympathetic nature," he said. "I knew you would have."

"How did you know? You know nothing about me."

"Ah, I know all I need to know." Shane looped his arm through hers and gave it a pat. "Let's get away from here."

She allowed him to guide her back to the main road and into a deserted alleyway.

"We mustn't miss the coach back," she reminded him, alarmed suddenly.

"Oh, we won't do that," he remarked confidently. "I just wanted to bring you somewhere where I can kiss you. I shall go mad if I don't."

She was taken aback for a moment and before she could rally her defences he had pulled her into his arms and planted a noisy kiss on her unsuspecting mouth.

She started to protest but he was kissing her again, his lips moving over hers in a sensuous manner so that she was rendered speechless.

He slowly let her go and they watched each other warily.

"What brought that on?" asked Romy flustered. She had not visualised Shane would have such a devastating effect on her senses and she was at a loss to explain the sudden surge of desire that stormed through her.

He was staring at her as if he saw her for the first time. "Romy . . . "

She slipped away from him and went towards the road again, frightened suddenly of her emotions. What was she doing allowing Shane to take liberties when it was Martin she liked? She must pull herself together. She had already had enough passion to last her a lifetime with Alex and she wasn't about to get into that situation again.

She saw Shane coming after her and headed across the road towards a coffee house. The place had a sweet, pungent smell.

She noticed all the customers were men. Some were playing dominoes and others were rolling dice.

Shane caught up with her inside. "I've heard about these coffee houses. They're a bit more than places to get a cup of coffee."

On the counter was a piece of gadgetry somewhere between a Russian samovar and a steam engine and it hissed and muttered.

Aware that all the men were staring at her, she sat down at a table and beckoned the waiter.

Balancing a full tray in one hand, he took their order for two coffees.

After they had been served with cups of the strong Arabic brew, Shane said, "I've just remembered. Coffee houses are strictly for the men."

She almost choked on her coffee. "But the waiter didn't say anything. And he took my order."

"It's probably only by custom and not by law."

"Oh, that's all right then." She giggled. "No wonder they all looked at me."

They saw the coach party across the road and Romy drained her cup.

"What's the hurry?" demanded Shane. "You just can't trust yourself to be alone with me, can you?"

"You're living in a dream world, Shane." She stood up. "Well I'm joining the others."

He took his time with his coffee then ambled after her. They spent the rest of the day in a museum looking at the remains of ancient Egypt.

Romy was thankful when she could at last scramble up the steps of the coach.

"What's up, Romy?" Shane slid into the seat beside her. "You and I could make wonderful music together."

She winced at the cliche. "Oh I don't think so."

"Well, I do. I think we've got a lot in common."

"How do you make that out?

"Well, you support Watford for a start."

"Look, Shane, I've had a nice time today." Romy leaned her head against the back of the seat. "Don't let's start getting serious. I've had serious up to here." She touched her chin.

He turned his gaze on her. "That

might be difficult. I could easily fall for you, Romy. To tell the truth I'm fed up with the old one-night-stand routine. I'm getting too old for that sort of thing. I warn you I'm looking for someone to settle down with."

"Well, don't look at me." She tried to sound indifferent. "The last thing I want to do is settle down. What, and lose all that lovely freedom!"

"You're in favour of one-night-stands then?"

"Those are not the only alternatives," she replied. "Have you never heard of couples who just loved each other?"

He scratched his head and grinned. "Can't say I have."

4

THEY arrived in Cairo in the early evening and stopped outside the hotel. Shane leapt down the coach steps and turned to hand Romy out. As her feet touched the tarmac, he pulled her into his arms and once more kissed her before she knew what was happening.

"Will you please stop doing that!" She tried to put a little venom in her voice but was aware she failed miserably.

"But you're so lovely I can't help myself."

"Yes, I knew it would turn out to be my fault."

"Ah! So that's what you get up to behind my back." Alex, who had just come out of a nearby shop, looked furious, despite his flippant tone.

Romy considered telling him to mind

his own business, but thought better of it. He was the director as she kept reminding herself and it wouldn't do any good to antagonise him more than was necessary.

She went into the hotel followed by Shane.

"He won't leave you alone, will he?" said the model, catching up with her. "How serious was it?"

"Quite serious." She took his arm as they approached the desk. "Actually I was crazily in love with him for rather a long time . . . "

Shane whistled softly. "Were you now! So that's the way the wind blows. What happened to sour the situation?"

"He was too possessive. I couldn't breathe."

"Well, I can understand him not wanting to let you go."

"Please, Shane, I don't want to talk about it." She couldn't think what madness had made her open her heart to Shane Shelley of all people. She reached the reception desk and held her hand out for her room key just as Martin stepped out of the lift.

"Did you have a nice day?" he asked, sounding more than a little put out.

"Oh, not you too!" she exclaimed, turning on her heel and making for the stairs. She immediately felt contrite. Martin didn't deserve to be spoken to like that. But she kept on going. She'd had enough of petty jealousies for one day and all she wanted to do was wallow in a hot bath.

As she reached her door she saw Sharon coming along the corridor.

"Did you hear about the money for the extras going missing?" she called.

"I did hear something about it," replied Romy putting her key in the lock. "Has it turned up yet?"

"No, they reckon it's been stolen. It's a nuisance. The extras are on strike and goodness knows when the filming will start again."

"Oh dear," said Romy. "It feels as if we'll we're stuck here ."

"I know," said Sharon. "But the

sheik has asked us round to the palace again so it can't be bad, can it?"

Romy went into her room just as the phone rang. Lifting the receiver she heard Shane's voice.

"It's most urgent that I speak with you. Can you meet me in the foyer in five minutes' time?"

"Oh Shane, can't it wait? I want to have a bath."

"Aw come on. It won't take long."

"Oh all right then," she grumbled. "But if this turns out to be a wild goose chase, heaven help you."

He was waiting just inside the door and as she crossed the foyer towards him he gripped her hands and practically swung her out through the revolving doors and into the sunshine.

"Romy, I've had a brilliant idea. Do you want to know what it is?"

"That's why I'm here."

"It'll surprise you. Do you want to sit down?"

"Oh for Pete's sake! Put it on fast forward, will you?"

"I've been giving it some serious thought. You and I should get married. We'll . . . "

"Hey, rewind that last bit."

"It's the logical solution to all your problems."

"How do make that out?" She laughed in his face. "I think marriage to you would double them."

For a split second he looked hurt, then he laughed grimly. "I was suggesting it to save you from Alex's clutches."

"Oh I see. A bit drastic, isn't it? And where does love come into all this, pray?"

"I could learn to love you." He pushed his fingers through his dark fringe in a helpless manner. "In fact I'm half-way there already."

She started to giggle. "Oh Shane, give over. You'll have me in hysterics in a minute."

"There's no talking to you," he said harshly. "I offer you marriage and you laugh in my face. Thanks!" And he turned and walked away.

Romy had an idea she had overlooked something vital But she couldn't think what. There were mysterious undertones here. She had obviously offended him. Goodness! The proposal wasn't for real, was it?

On reflection she rather thought it was. Well, well, Shane had proposed to her.

And she had laughed in his face.

* * *

The money for the extras was still missing and they continued refusing to work. Alex had sent to London for more money but it had not arrived yet so he had no choice but to grant the crew another day off.

Once again Sheik Abu Ben Talin put his palace at their disposal and Romy took time out to make friends with his daughter, Tanita. She had brought her small travelling beauty case with her and, with the sheik's permission, proceeded to paint the little girl's face and turn her into a clown.

Romy, Tanita and the nurse were in the walled rose garden with the heady perfume of thousands of blooms surrounding them.

As she worked on Tanita's face Romy wondered if the child was lonely. She must be. Her father was so frightened of kidnappers he had told her that he daren't let her mix with children of her own age unless their families were carefully vetted. It seemed a shame; she had so many advantages living in a palace and having servants to wait on her hand and foot but she could not be free. She obviously didn't find it irksome to have a nurse with her all the time but she may well resent it when she was older. It wouldn't suit Romy.

The nurse was a quiet little thing dressed in an unbecoming brown robe with a hood that almost covered her face. Her name was Favori and from the little Romy could see of her, she guessed she was in her early forties.

Tanita was delighted when Romy had finished painting and she clapped her hands with delight while Romy held the mirror. She could speak quite a few words of English and said, "Me go show daddy."

She ran off towards the palace with her nurse in hot pursuit and Romy took a stroll through the garden. There were numerous species of roses and she recognised a lot of British ones. She was surprised to see so many different trees beyond the little wrought iron gate and remembered being told that the sheik had imported trees from all over the world.

All at once she heard voices. A man and a woman were talking urgently the other side of the wall. Probably the gardeners. It sounded very emotional but you never could tell. People from the Middle East were wont to make crises out of dramas. Romy was never averse to a bit of eavesdropping but they weren't speaking in English so she couldn't understand what was being said.

It sounded a mite sinister and she wondered if the sheik knew they were there. Recalling his anxiety over the prospect of Tanita being kidnapped she thought she'd better report it. She walked briskly across the lawns towards the palace.

Rounding a corner she saw Tanita hand in hand with a young man whom she had never seen before. Dressed in pink teeshirt and blue-jeans, he had a mop of untidy black hair, long sideburns and his face was covered in scars.

Of the nurse there was no sign.

Romy had a premonition of danger. She ran forward and asked, "Who are you? How did you get in?"

As she spoke she was grabbed from behind. Whoever it was had hold of her was strong and the fingers dug in like talons. There was also a powerful smell of garlic. She half-turned her head and saw it was another dark-haired young man similarly attired with glasses and a full black beard.

Romy thought they didn't look Egyptian, thety were more the Latin-type. Probably Spanish she decided.

The man holding her spoke first in Arabic then, seeing her blank expression, switched to English, heavily accented. "Keep you mouth shut!" He gave her arms a violent twist which brought tears to her eyes. "Do you see what I have here?" And he produced from his pocket a lethal-looking knife. He added, "And I'm not afraid to use it."

Tanita started to cry.

"Shut up!" he shouted.

His colleague shot his a warning glance. "You'd better take some of that advice for yourself, Enricho. Do you want us to be caught red-handed."

The other ignored his outburst and continued to speak to Tanita in English; "You be a good little girl and I won't have to hurt you."

She gave a loud shriek and burst into

heart-wrenching tears.

Her captor shook her till her teeth rattled but only succeeded in making her cry all the more.

"Oh please," said Romy. "Don't hurt her. Let her come to me."

"You are in no position to demand anything," said the man called Enricho. He added ominously, "But if she doesn't stop crying I shall stop her."

Romy knelt beside the child and put her arms about her. "It's all right, Tanita, I'm here with you." The make-up had started to run and the little girl's face was a colourful mess.

Over her shoulder Romy said, "What do you want?"

"All in good time," said Enricho. He seized Romy's arm and dragged her into the shadows of the trees. The scarred man picked up Tanita, none too gently, and followed.

When he had caught up with them he thrust his burden into Romy's arms. "Here, take her." He turned. "Follow me."

At that moment Favori arrived, flushed from running. She saw what was happening to Tanita and uttered a stream of Arabic. Romy gathered from her limited knowledge of the language that she was scolding the child for giving her the slip like that. She had obviously not taken the scene in yet. When she did, she became almost hysterical.

The scarred man seized her and brandished his knife against her neck. She began to scream and the two men exchanged anxious glances.

"Stop her, can't you," said Enricho. "We'll have the whole palace down on us in a moment."

Whereupon the other suddenly brought up his fist and dealt the nurse a heavy blow on the top of her head. She crumpled to the ground and lay there very still.

"You've killed her," gasped Romy.

"Pedro! You fool!" said the bearded man.

Pedro knelt beside Favori and felt

her pulse. "She lives." He spoke with no compassion or emotion and Romy shivered.

He picked Favori up and slung her over his shoulder as if she were a bag of laundry. "Come on!"

Romy held Tanita close and accompanied the two men along the tree-lined path until they came to a parked Ford Transit van with the name of a dry cleaning company on the side.

A redhaired woman of European appearance and dressed in black was in the driving seat, scowling as the group approached. She looked ten years older than the men — both of whom appeared to be in their late twenties — and was obviously in charge. Romy noticed she had what looked like a falcon tattooed on the back of her hand.

"Quickly, quickly. We haven't got all day." She hurled the words in the men's direction as they made their way towards her. She spoke in Spanish of which Romy had a grounding although she pretended not to understand.

"What have you brought her for?" She indicated Romy.

"We had no choice," grumbled Pedro. "She knows too much."

"And what's the matter with the kid? Her face . . . " The woman looked startled. "Is it catching."

"Stage make-up," said Pedro with a wry grin.

Romy, Tanita and Favori were bundled into the back of the van in which there were no windows. The scarred man held his hand over Tanita's mouth so that her crying was muffled.

The woman drove forward.

"One word from you and the kid can say goodbye to her fifth birthday." The words sounded comical, like in a film, but Romy couldn't fail to detect the sinister undertones. She clamped her mouth shut, it was the only way to ensure she didn't breathe a word.

At the gates to the palace two guards came forward and one, chewing gum, gave a cursory look into the van and waved them on.

They hurtled into the appalling traffic and sped towards the city centre with the woman driving like a madman, the silence inside the car broken only by Favori's weeping. As they reached the old city walls the woman brought the van to a halt.

"Easy!" she said, taking a long cigarette holder from the glove compartment and fixing a small cigar to it.

She turned to Romy and snarled in English, "Now you go back to the sheik and tell him if he wants to see his daughter again he must carry out my instructions to the letter." She took hold of the lapels of Romy's blouse and brought her face to within an inch of hers. Romy tried not to reel away from the foul smell of the woman's breath.

"Listen carefully. Tomorrow the sheik will go to all the jewellers' shops in Cairo and thereabouts and purchase uncut diamonds to the value of . . . " She mentioned an amount in

Egyptian pounds which was equal to a million pounds in English money. "He will put them in this." She produced a nondescript canvas bag and handed it to Romy.

Turning to Favori, who had recovered consciousness by now, she blew cigar smoke into her face and said: "You can drive a car."

Favori started to deny it.

"We have been watching you and we know you can drive."

Favori shrugged helplessly.

"You, yes you!" She jabbed the nurse's chest. "You will take the diamonds to an address I will give you over the phone. You will tell no one. If the police are informed the child will die. Now have you got that?"

Favori nodded sulkily.

The redhead said with undeniable pride, "The Falcon has spoken."

Romy vaguely recalled having read somewhere about a gang of terrorists calling themselves the Falcon.

The car spun round and sped

back towards the palace, stopping outside. Roughly Romy and Favori were bundled out. Romy fell heavily grazing her knee on the sharp grit of the road and knocking her elbow on the rear mudguard.

She heard Tanita scream. "It's all right, dear," she called, scrambling to her feet, "Your daddy will come and get you . . . "

A minute later the van was a tiny speck in the distance.

Romy ran to help Favori to her feet. The woman was in a bad state of nerves and her crying was becoming ragged.

"I can't drive to the meeting place. I have only driven round the palace," she sobbed, "I will let you all down."

Romy gave her a swift hug. "Come on, we've got to tell the sheik the terrible news."

The crying increased. "And I can't face Abu Ben Talid. He will be heartbroken."

"Don't worry, I shall tell him." Romy

threaded her arm through Favori's and they hastened to the gates of the palace where they were recognised and admitted.

The sheik was in his study, one of servants told them. Romy rapped on the door and turned the handle to see him pacing the floor. "May I have a word . . . " she began.

He spun round and bounded towards her. "Thank heavens you've come! Is Tanita with you?"

"No," said Romy who couldn't think of way to break it to him gently. "She's been . . . kidnapped."

The expression on his face was one of sheer horror. He strode to the phone on his desk and lifted the receiver.

Romy sprang forward. "No!"

Favori was still in shock and was making a lot of noise with her crying so Romy had to shout. She quickly explained what had happened and told him about the arrangements for paying the ransom.

"So you see, you mustn't call the

police," she finished.

He bade them be seated and then asked Favori if she could add anything, but was met with another flood of tears.

His face as white as the robes he wore, the sheik suddenly let out a strangled groan and held his head in his hands. "What am I going to do?"

He seemed to have completely gone to pieces.

Romy stretched out her hand and gently touched his shoulder. "Can you raise the money for the diamonds?"

The sheik visibly pulled himself together. "Yes, it will take a little time." He began to pace the floor again. "And my credit standing is good."

He walked briskly to the door and shouted for his secretary. A moment later an elderly man, in western dress, entered. Romy had seen him before and knew he had earned respect for his outstanding work over the years in the sheik's father's days. Because of this he was always addressed formally as Mr Pimerik. She saw he immediately sensed the tension in the room and took out his notepad.

"Sit down," said the sheik grimly, "and listen to what Romy has to say." He glanced in her direction. "Would you mind saying it all again, my dear."

She opened her mouth to begin but it had gone dry.

"Oh, do forgive me," said Ben Talid, "You must be thirsty." He pressed a buzzer on his desk and asked for a jug of lemonade to be brought to the study.

In the meantime Romy reiterated the events of the morning.

When the lemonade arrived a few minutes later she saw it was homemade. The sheik poured her a generous glassfull and she was taken back to her childhood by the taste.

The secretary was asked to locate all the jewellers' shops in the vicinity. He would have a formidable task. The trouble was they did not know how much time they had. The crucial phone call could come at any moment.

"Don't you think you should tell the police?" asked Mr Pimerik. "They are better equipped for dealing with this sort of thing."

"No!" exclaimed Romy. "The woman seemed quite ruthless. I really believe she would carry out her threat to harm Tanita. And that man, that Pedro, has a vicious streak in him. The way he lashed out at Favori was quite uncalled for. I admit I thought he had killed her."

The sheik stroked his chin looking undecided.

"But the police would be discreet, I'm sure," said the secretary, not willing seemingly to let go of the idea. "They will visit you out of uniform so, if the kidnappers are watching, they will not connect them with the police."

"That's not strictly true," argued the sheik. "You can usually spot a policeman a mile off. No, I'm inclined to agree with Romy."

"But so much money," muttered the secretary.

"Exactly. It's only money." Ben Talid picked up a photograph of Tanita, laughing as she rode a pony. He smiled fondly at it. It was a good and recent likeness and as he gazed at it a tear replaced the smile.

"But my little girl is a jewel among jewels." He looked boldly at the others and Romy sensed he had made up his mind. "Diamonds they want, so diamonds they shall have."

The secretary left to go about his task and the sheik picked up the phone once more to summon his chauffeur. Then he looked thoughtfully at Favori. "I know you can drive but I don't think you are capable of taking the ransom."

"I'll do it," offered Romy recklessly.

"But they have stipulated Favori . . ." began the sheik.

"Ah, you're forgetting I'm a make-up artist." She gave a hint of a smile. "I imagine it will be quite straightforward disguising myself as Favori. Besides she wears covering clothes."

The sheik looked doubtful. "I don't know . . . "

"Well, it's one solution if all else fails," said Romy. "I imagine you will think of others. Just call on me if you need me. I mean it."

"Thank you, Romy, my dear." He noticed the Rolls had come to park outside the window and strode towards the door. "Now I must leave you and go and buy some diamonds."

The door closed behind him and Romy went to comfort Favori.

"Don't worry," she murmured in her schoolgirl Arabic. "You won't have to drive with the diamonds You're too highly strung for the sheik to risk it. No? I bet you a penny to a pound I will be the one."

Favori stopped crying. Although she hadn't understood one word of what Romy had said she sensed from her tone that everything was all right.

Romy felt she ought to hang on a bit in case the phone call came and she was asked to drive.

But the hours passed with no word from the sheik or the kidnappers. She sought the secretary out and told him she was going back to the hotel but that they call on her any time to fulfil her promise.

The first thing on the agenda when she got back was a long wallow in a hot bath She was sitting on the edge of the bed using the hair-dryer. when there came a tap on the door.

"Come in," she called, "It's not locked."

It was Shane. "What's up, Romy?" He watched her anxiously. "You looked ghastly when you came in."

"The sheik's little girl has been kidnapped." She switched off the dryer and threw it on the bed. "I was witness to it all. In fact I thought I was kidnapped too."

"You poor kid." He sat beside her on the bed and put an arm loosely around her shoulders. "Tell me more."

His presence was strangely comforting. As she told her story yet again he listened carefully, nodding at intervals.

When she had finished he was quiet for a moment then he said passionately, "You can't possibly drive the car with the ransom money. It's too dangerous. Better let me do it."

"No, Shane, I've already told the sheik I will do it. Besides it has to be a female." Her face broke into a mischievous grin. "And no way can I disguise you as a girl."

He didn't smile. "It's not on. I won't allow you to risk your pretty neck."

"You won't allow it?" Her laugh sounded brittle. "It's not up to you."

"Oh, isn't it? We'll see about that." He jutted his chin stubbornly. "I don't think Alex will be pleased if you're called away in the middle of filming."

"Oh please, don't tell Alex. The least people who know about this the better. Ben Talid doesn't want the press or the police to get wind of it."

"So you've got to hang around near the phone for goodness knows how long."

"That's no hardship. And the call won't come through today. The kidnappers will be sure to give the sheik time to get the diamonds. They're not stupid."

Shane chewed his lower lip thoughtfully. "I may have a plan."

"Please don't interfere, Shane. You'll only foul things up."

He wasn't listening. He rose abruptly and went out.

Romy dressed in a linen two-piece, the colour of old pewter and went downstairs. Now she had had time to think about it she regretted her impulsiveness in offering to stand in for Favori. It was madness to think she had the courage to go through with it She would be so frightened she would probably put the whole rescue mission in jeopardy. But she had given her word and there could be no going back. Despite the heat she shivered.

"Cold?" It was Martin downstairs in the foyer.

"Oh hello, Martin. No, I just had one of those funny feelings, like someone walking over my grave."

"What you want is a drink." He steered her towards the bar. "A large whisky should do the trick."

"No thanks, Martin. I've got to keep a clear head. I might be called on to drive a car any moment now." As soon as the words were out she could have bitten her tongue. Now she would have to tell Martin. She had already told Shane that the sheik wanted it kept secret and here she was telling everybody she met. She might as well rent some time on television and broadcast it to the nation.

She filled him in on the main points and swore him to secrecy. "If too many people get to know about it, it's certain to get to the ears of the police," she explained, "and they'll insist on taking over. But the kidnappers stipulated no police."

"Of course they did," said Martin. "Because they know the game would be up. And that's why the police should be called in."

"But the sheik doesn't want them, not yet anyway. It's only fair to let him try his way first."

He bought her a large pineapple juice and a lager for himself and carried the drinks out to the garden.

"I don't like to think of you driving that car," he said when they had chosen a rustic table with chairs around it beneath the trees. "It's no job for a woman."

"Well, that's a sexist remark if ever I heard one," admonished Romy, lifting her glass. "We're on a par with men now when it comes to dangerous jobs."

"Ah yes, forgive me." He smiled gently. "I wasn't looking at you as a woman but a friend, a very dear friend."

"Why, Martin, how nice of you." Only a friend? she thought disconsolately.

They sat smiling at each other till a

waiter came out with a mobile phone and told Romy she had a call.

She took it gingerly as if it might turn into something nasty.

But it was Alex and he sounded drunk.

"Romy, you're driving me crazy. Gimme a little break, won't you?"

She held the handset away from her ear, but she could still hear him. "Listen, Alex, I've no intention of giving you any breaks, big or little." And she pushed in the aerial and handed it back to the waiter.

It was a strange old world, she mused. There was Alex supposedly in love with her, and Shane trying to imagine himself in love with her, and all she wanted was Martin with whom she was getting nowhere.

It was not until the evening two days later when the call that Romy had been dreading came.

She'd had a busy day on the set and fallen foul of Alex's tongue several times. She had felt like telling him to go to hell, but managed somehow to resist the urge.

As she had heard nothing she presumed Favori had been up to the job of driving after all.

They hadn't been invited to the palace since the kidnap scare and Romy was sitting in the games room, watching Martin and Shane playing ping-pong when the waiter brought the phone again.

With her heart beating so loudly she was sure the others could hear it, she said, "Hello?"

"Hello, Romy," answered Abu Ben Talid. "I'm afraid we have need of the services you so kindly offered. Favori has completely broken down. Does your offer still stand?"

His voice contained a deep sadness which tore at her emotions. She couldn't have said no if she'd tried. What that poor man must be going through.

She smoothed the skirt of her spice-coloured dress. "Yes."

"Thank you, my dear." He gave a deep sigh of relief. "Will you come to the palace? I'll send a car."

She put down the handset and forced a smile. "Well, this is it. It's a good job filming has finished for the day."

"I'm coming with you," Shane announced, throwing his bat onto the table.

"Same here," said Martin.

"You're both going to ruin the whole thing." Romy stood up and went to the tall window to watch out for the car. "Is there anything I can do to stop you?"

They both shook their heads and Shane said, "There's no need for you to come, Martin. I can handle it."

"Oh yeah!" sneered Martin. "What suddenly makes you a hero? Why, you can't even blow your nose without me holding the hankie."

It sounded to Romy as if they were sparring over her. This was not the time for quarrels. "Shut up, both of you. I'm just going to fetch my bag of tricks and I'll be ready."

She paused in the doorway. "And I don't want to find you fighting when I get back."

Shane gave a sloppy salute. "No ma'am."

She ran to her room and grabbed her make-up case. It was quite heavy. When she reached the foyer, Martin was keeping watch from the window.

"Nice timing," he said, taking the case. "The sheik's Rolls is just turning into the courtyard."

"Talk about style!" muttered Shane. He took her hand and squeezed it. Quietly he said, "If you knew what you're putting me through you'd quit now."

She sensed he was being serious and felt him tremble. Looking into his eyes she read there a message of deep concern for her safety, so unexpected that she experienced a brief rush of desire for him. It was quite out of keeping with the task that faced her and she hastily glanced away.

Martin said, “Well come on, don’t keep the chauffeur waiting.”

The three of them piled onto the back seat and the car headed for the palace.

5

THE sheik was in the palace gardens watching out for them. He looked so forlorn that Romy's heart went out to him. What he must have gone through since they had last seen him did not bear thinking about.

A look of surprise spread over his face as he saw the two men step out of the car.

"It's okay," said Romy, "They've only come for the ride."

"Now look here," said Shane. "I don't approve of this plan to use Romy."

"But she offered . . . "

"She's a kindhearted girl," butted in Martin.

"Well, I'm sorry . . . really I am . . . " Abu Ben stared Romy in the face. "It's not such a good idea then?"

"Yes it is," cried Romy. "I'm prepared to honour my promise. Take no notice of these two. I've suddenly acquired some bodyguards." She turned to address them. "Get this straight. I'm going to do this impersonation and nobody's going to stop me. If you've only come along to put a spanner in the works you can leave now."

Martin opened and shut his mouth while Shane grimaced. They both fell in step behind Romy as the sheik led them to his study. There were several small black sacks made of velvet on the desk which Romy assumed contained the diamonds. She had no idea what a million pounds' worth of diamonds looked like so she could not gauge whether or not the sheik had been successful in obtaining the full amount.

The secretary, Mr Pimerik, was already in the room and he smiled grimly as they entered. "Thank goodness you've come. Abu Ben has been out of his mind with worry."

The sheik indicated the sacks. "It's all there, you'll be interested to know."

"Have the kidnappers been in touch with you?" asked Romy.

"They telephoned an hour ago and Mr Pimerik has it all written down for you."

The secretary passed her a sheet of paper and she read it aloud: "'This is The Falcon,' Do you know anything about this Falcon?"

Romy shook her head.

"They are a gang of international terrorists. They deal in drug trafficking and money laundering plus anything else that shows a profit." His eyes went to the letter again. "'If you want to see your daughter alive you will follow these instructions to the letter. At precisely eight o'clock today the nurse will drive 30 kilometres along the Shari Ramses road. Just before she gets to the end of it she will turn right. She will drive one hundred metres to the second turning on the right. She will get out of the car and go to the phone box on the corner and wait for further instructions. She will have the diamonds with her. If you inform the police or in any way seek to discover our identity your daughter will be killed instantly. Believe me.'"

Romy had gone very pale and Shane took her hand. "Are you sure? You only have to say the word. No-one will think badly of you."

She recovered her poise and shook his hand away. "How many times must I tell you . . . " She saw his face fall and realised she was being ill-mannered. He only had her wellbeing in mind. "Oh, I'm sorry, Shane. I know you are only trying to help, but I'm all right, honestly I am."

"Well, I don't like it."

"So you keep saying." She gave a deep sigh of exasperation and concentrated on the sheik. "So I've got an hour to turn myself into Favori."

"I'll send for her," said Mr Pimerik and he busied himself with the intercom.

When Favori appeared it was plain

she had been weeping. "I have let everybody down," she said.

"Don't you worry about a thing," crooned Romy. "I shall do the run, just as soon as I've turned myself into you."

The nurse looked bemused.

"You'll see."

Romy opened her case and took out several sticks of make-up. She sat Favori down on a chair and started to disguise herself as the brown-skinned woman, using a sable base and sallow highliner.

"We might as well leave the ladies to it," said the sheik. "Come, gentlemen, let us take a stroll around the garden."

Romy was glad they had gone. She was self-conscious with them looking on.

She put the sable base on her arms and legs then sent Favori for one of her spare robes.

She heard the men returning and gesticulated to Favori to stand behind the door. Then she dropped into the chair the nurse had vacated.

Shane came in first closely followed Martin, the sheik and Mr Pimerik.

The sheik peered round the room and asked the figure on the chair, "Hello, where's Romy?"

Romy smiled and answered, "She's right here, gentlemen."

The three men gaped at her. "Can it be true?" asked the sheik. Whereupon Favori stepped from behind the door.

"Well, I would never have believed it!" exclaimed the sheik. "You have certainly put my mind at rest."

Martin pulled a face. "That's all very well if you don't have to get out of the car."

"And your Arabic isn't so hot," Shane pointed out. "You won't understand the further instructions over the phone."

"I know enough to get by." She glanced at her watch. "It's nearly eight o'clock. Oo-er!"

At once Martin put an arm around her. "My dear Romy. You're being rather pigheaded. Can't you see I'm worried sick about you?"

She thrust his arm away impatiently. "I've had enough of this." To the sheik she said, "Shall we put the diamonds in the car?"

Mr Pimerik went to the desk and gathered up the little velvet sacks. "It pains me to hand all this wealth to a bunch of crooks. I still think you should have called in the police."

"No, I'm sure this is the right way to deal with these sort of people. They have no moral fibre and won't have any qualms about killing Tanita." Abu Ben almost choked as he spoke his daughter's name.

He took out a large pocket watch and studied it for a moment. Romy thought he was in a trance. Or perhaps he was praying. He jerked his head upwards. "Right! Let's get this show on the road."

His use of American slang seemed oddly out of place but it served to break the tension in the room.

Romy picked up her long skirts and

made to follow but Shane stepped in front of her. "Romy, please!"

There was something about him that made her tremble and it had nothing to do with the task that lay ahead of her. For a moment time seemed to stand still as she gazed at him. All at once, despite the traumatic events of the past few minutes, she sensed a great burst of desire well up inside her and she had to fight down an urge to throw herself into his arms. To cover her confusion she said, "Give over, Shane!"

She carried on after the sheik out to the rear courtyard where a car awaited them. It wasn't the Rolls but a sturdy little *Lada Samara*.

The sheik explained. "If you turn up in an expensive car they might decide to keep it and you'd have no transport home. And here is some petty cash. You might have to use the phone or take a taxi or something."

He seemed to have thought of everything.

While Romy climbed into the driver's

seat and familiarised herself with the controls, Mr Pimerik took up the holdall the redhaired woman had given to Romy, and transferred the diamonds to it. With a sigh of resignation he handed it to her.

The sheik put his head through the open window. "It's a very reliable little car and there's a full tank of petrol so you won't run out." He kissed Romy's cheek. "I am eternally in your debt."

She turned her head to wave to her two 'bodyguards' but only Martin stood there.

"Good luck!" he shouted.

Romy had already been briefed about the route she must take and swung the car onto the Shari Ramses road. She couldn't fail to find it for it was clearly signposted.

The traffic was atrocious as always. She had to take care not to hit the jaywalkers who were everywhere and the cars came towards her from all directions. She was reminded of that old joke 'in London you drive on the left, in New York on the right but in Cairo it's optional'.

With the instructions on the seat beside her, she drove the thirty kilometres to the turning just before the road merged with another, then took the road on the right. As she swerved to miss a jay-walker, something caught her eye. She glanced in her mirror and was so appalled to see Shane sitting on the back seat, she almost lost control of the car.

"That's better," he said cheerfully. "It was making my neck ache crouching down there between the seats."

"What on earth do you think you're doing?" she demanded bringing the car out of a stall. "The crooks might have me under surveillance. If they see you they're going to be pretty sore."

"Relax," he murmured lazily. "No way was I going to let you make this journey alone."

She sighed. She had a Sir Galahad on her hands and there was nothing she could do about it.

"For goodness sake, keep out of sight!"

He leaned back against the seat and slid down a little. "This okay?"

"I suppose it'll have to be."

She had driven the thirty metres to the second turning on the right and there was the phone box on the corner.

Shane ducked down between the seats again and Romy got out.

Night falls fast in the desert and the blackness seemed to envelope her totally. The only light came from the phone box.

It was a lonely road — it must be the least congested in Cairo — and she could just make out fields of stubble on either side of her. All was still and silent.

She stood there for five minutes then she heard the phone ring.

She hastened into the box. It was like an old-fashioned English kiosk with a heavy door.

Grabbing the receiver off the hook

she said in her best Arabic, "It is I, Favori."

A man's voice said, "This is the Falcon. Listen carefully. You will leave the diamonds in the left luggage office at Cairo airport. You will leave the key in an envelope, addressed to Mr Falcon, at the messages counter. You will get out fast. Do you understand?"

"Yes." she gulped and the phone went dead.

She went to the car and told Shane what she had to do.

When they reached the airport she said, "They'll be watching every move I make so you'd better make yourself scarce."

He got down between the seats again and she took up the holdall.

"I hope to be back in a minute or two," she said, her voice shaking.

"You'd better be," came Shane's muffled reply.

The place was crowded.

The left luggage section was just inside the terminal and she carried out her instructions, putting the holdall in one of the vacant lockers, feeding money in and locking it.

Next she went to the messages desk. There was a pile of unused envelopes and she slipped the key into one. She borrowed a pen from the clerk and wrote the name 'Mr Falcon'.

After paying the sum the clerk demanded she 'got out fast'.

Returning to the car park she discovered Shane was no longer in the car. Wherever he was she supposed she had better wait for him. She climbed in and leaned her head back. As the tension subsided within her she realised she was shaking like a leaf.

An hour passed and she wondered what Shane could be doing. She couldn't wait there indefinitely. Figuring that the kidnappers had redeemed the key and were well on their way, she went back to the airport lounge. There were even more people about now and she was jostled on all sides. She couldn't see Shane anywhere even though she climbed on a bench. He must have followed the Falcon and could be anywhere, on a plane even.

She didn't know what to do for the best. In the end she left a note with the clerk at the messages desk, to the effect that she had gone back to the palace if anyone asked for her by name.

Outside in the car-park she didn't see the woman kidnapper until it was too late.

The redhead grabbed Romy's arm and hissed, in Arabic, "You little double-crosser! You were not alone."

Romy decided to tell the truth and just in time remembered to speak in Arabic. "I didn't know he was there until I was on the way. I tried to get rid of him."

The woman was studying her intently. Romy knew she was sweating profusely and guessed the make-up must be running.

She turned towards the car. Before

she could escape she was seized from behind.

She was aware that it was a man who had here in his grasp. Before anything could register a soft damp cloth was placed over her mouth and it was the last thing she knew.

* * *

Romy woke in a small windowless room that was sparsely furnished apart from several large boxes stacked in one corner. She was lying on the floor and there was a bitter taste in her mouth. She wanted to be sick. She was alone and as the events of the day came swiftly back to her she wondered what had happened to the gang of kidnappers and Shane and Tanita. It seemed likely that Shane had also been captured.

She stood up shakily and tried the door. As she had thought it was locked but it had been worth a try. She looked at her watch and seeing it was midnight realised she had been unconscious for over an hour. She banged on the door and shouted in Arabic. "Help! Let me out."

She pressed her ear to the door and heard a slight scuffling noise then a key turning in the lock. Moments later the door swung open and the man she knew as Pedro stood there. He was pointing a small revolver in her direction.

With his free hand he touched her cheek and then held up his fingers to show her the make-up stain. "Very clever," he sneered. "But you can't fool me."

"I didn't want to fool you," she said, "I didn't want to fool anybody." Speaking Arabic was becoming a strain and as there was no need to keep up the pretence any longer she lapsed into English. "I had to drive the car. Favori was too scared."

"No matter," he said with a shrug. "Now that you are conscious I have orders to feed you. I must lock the door again while I go and fetch the food."

"I don't want anything to eat . . ." she began.

"But you will be wanting a drink? No?"

"No!" She continued to taste the bitterness in her mouth. "Yes . . . please."

He locked the door and she heard his footsteps receding. A moment later he was back with a large glass jug of water

As she held it to her lips and took a great swig she was weighing up the pros and cons of hitting him with the jug in order to escape. But before that she must find out where Tanita was.

"What have you done with the little girl?"

"She is safe. We are not barbarians. You will get her back when we have had the diamonds valued and we have removed ourselves from the country."

He had dropped his guard and put the revolver in his belt. She put the jug to her mouth again and suddenly lunged forward. It caught him on the side of his head with an almighty crack. As he went down blood spurted from his nose.

Romy bent to take the revolver and stuffed it under her robe before stepping over his still form.

She went out of the door and locked it and then she was running for all she was worth along a corridor and up some stone steps to another door, beyond which she could hear voices.

Drawing the revolver, she stealthily turned the door handle. It opened. Enricho was pacing the floor talking to the redhead who was seated in an armchair. She heard him address her as Stefana.

The room was shabby, but gave an impression of having been well-appointed in days gone by. There was a marble fireplace and bell ropes for calling the servants and the furniture was old and heavy.

All this Romy took in at a glance.

"Do you know what I'd like to do?" Stefana was saying. "After we've finished the other business? I'd like to torture that interfering English girl and kill her." She rubbed her hands together and smiled a grisly smile. "I hate those stuck-up little blondes. I'd make her wish she'd never been born."

Her tone made Romy's blood run cold.

Romy had the advantage of surprise and took it. Brandishing the weapon she ran forward and ordered them to lie face down on the floor. They were so surprised they did what she said without question.

As the woman recovered her senses she swore at Romy in all the languages she knew.

"Be quiet!" snapped Romy. "I'm calling the tune now."

It sounded so bizarre to her ears that she almost laughed. But it was no laughing matter. She stepped over their inert bodies and opened a further door keeping the revolver trained on them. She flung herself through the doorway, closed it smartly and carried on running.

Coming to an ornate staircase and. aware of sounds of pursuit, she fairly flew up it. She knew in films the heroine always ran away up the stairs instead of down and was caught, but she wanted to find out if Shane was on the premises.

Coming to a landing with three doors, she tried them all. All were unlocked so she did not think Tanita or Shane would be incarcerated there.

There was a small flight of stairs at the end of the corridor which plainly led to the attic. Holding up her cumbersome skirts she bounded up them. One door faced her. It was locked.

"Tanita! Shane! Are you in there?" She pounded on the door.

"What kept you?" came Shane's laid-back voice.

To her surprise and delight the key

was still in the door. A moment later she had released him. There was no Tanita.

She rushed into his arms, laughing and crying at the same time.

"I didn't know you cared," he quipped, holding her away from him. "There's no time that." He lowered his voice to a vibrant burr. "I'll see you later."

She briefly explained what had happened and that her pursuers were hot on her tail.

Shane darted back in the room and emerged with an iron fender. It looked heavy. "Follow me," he said, creeping towards the top of the stairs.

Enricho and Stefana were halfway up the flight. Shane charged down laying about them with the fender. They both tried to escape him. Enricho fell back and rolled to the bottom of the stairs where he lay still. Stefana knelt down and covered her head with her arms then lost her footing and rolled down after her colleague.

Shane grabbed Romy's hand. "Come on! I know where Tanita is! I watched them from the window. They've put her in a sort of shed at the back of the house."

Shane led Romy outside to an outhouse and before she could catch her breath he had broken down the door. From the smell of the interior it was used for drying herbs.

Romy could see through the gloom, Tanita lying wide awake on a bed of straw.

"Tanita! My poor baby." She lifted her up and cuddled her. "It's me! Romy. Although I'm dressed as Favori, which is a bit confusing for you."

Tanita clung to her for dear life. She still wore traces of the clown make-up that Romy had used and looked as if she had cut herself. Romy made sure that was not the case.

"They didn't even have the decency to wash her face," she said.

"Stop waffling." Shane spoke tersely. "Those crooks will catch up with us any moment. We don't stand a dog's chance in hell."

"Sounds like defeatist talk to me." Romy held the child closer. "What do you think, Tanita?"

Tanita tried to raise a smile but didn't quite make it.

They raced through the long narrow yard and came to bolted and chained gate. Shane looked round for something to use as a lever and came up with a another fender. Between them they managed to force the gate open. It was no good, there was another yard and heavy gate beyond it. The fender was useless. Surrounding this yard was a high wall.

"Defeatist talk, eh?" Shane grated out. "Right, you asked for it!" He took a running jump at the wall and managed to get a finger-hold in a crevice near the top. By stretching and angling his long legs about he was able to scale the wall. He perched on the top and reached his arms down for Tanita. "Pass her up to me."

"Oh, I don't know . . . "

"Come on! What are you hanging about for? Do you want them to catch us or not?"

She made up her mind in a rush and shoved Tanita in his direction. The child was wriggling but Shane seized her by her clothes and hauled her up into his lap.

"You're next!"

"But you've got your hands full already."

"I'm glad you noticed." He leaned down and touched her shoulder.

She knew she had to get out of this yard. The sound of someone approaching was getting nearer. It was a matter of moments before the door burst open and they were recaptured. She gave herself up to him.

He lifted her as easily as if she were a rag doll. She could feel his muscles straining and smelt his perspiration. She was so near him she felt him almost smothering her.

After he had her safely in his lap

he pushed her over the other side of the wall onto a convenient bench. Tanita followed and finally Shane leapt down.

He scooped Tanita into his arms and raced off along the road. Romy followed as fast as her cumbersome clothes would allow.

The traffic was speeding by under bright lamp lights. By some stroke of good fortune there was a taxi for hire and Shane hailed it. As they piled in they looked back and saw the three kidnappers come haring through the gate and stare around.

"We made it!" said Shane. "There were times there when I didn't think we were going to." He glanced Romy. "My dear, how are we going to convince everybody we really did this fantastic thing? Even I don't believe it."

"Well, we've got Tanita to prove it."

"Yes, we've certainly got Tanita." He kissed the child's dark head.

"You haven't told me yet how

you got into this mess," said Romy accusingly.

"It's a long story and will sound far-fetched." He looked thoughtful. "I doubt I'd believe it if such a story was told to me."

"Try me," she said and, when he still hesitated, "Oh for goodness sake tell me what happened?" she cried impatiently.

He grinned infuriatingly. "You look lovely when you get all stroppy like that." He saw her glower at him. "Okay. Well, I got out of the car while you were in the airport."

"I know that, you fool!"

"Look, are you going to let me tell this story in my own way?"

"Sorry." She knew she didn't sound it.

"I didn't even get to the counter before one of the gang came up behind me and shoved a gun in my ribs. He must have seen me get out of the car, so he knew I was with you. He ordered me outside to the car park where another man was waiting. They bundled me into a van and blindfolded me before they drove off. The rest must be pretty much the same as happened to you, I imagine."

"More or less." Romy caught sight of her reflection in the window and groaned. Her robe was torn and dirty and the sable make-up had run and streaked her face like war paint. "What a sight I look! You might have said!" she exclaimed. Her hand went straight to her hair. "Will it ever be clean again? I look like refugee from hell." She stared at her companions, at Tanita's clown face and Shane's dusty profile. "And you two don't look much better. It's a wonder the cabbie picked us up."

"Whatever we look like, the sheik is going to regard us as a sight for sore eyes." Shane, sitting with Tanita on his lap, ruffled her dark hair. "Yes, I reckon he's going to be mighty pleased. He'll probably recommend me for the royal order of the salmon tin."

Romy laughed. "I know life is never dull making these commercials, but this is ridiculous." She looked obliquely at him. "That really was an adventure and none of it would have happened if it hadn't been for you. You wouldn't have been captured, and I wouldn't have hung around waiting for you and so get captured myself." On a sudden impulse she leaned across and kissed his cheek. "I'm so thankful you went against the sheik's wishes and insisted on coming though."

They arrived at the palace and the guard at the gate gasped with surprise when he saw Tanita with them. The sheik had obviously told the guards; about the kidnapping for security reasons.

Shane asked the man not to tell the sheik as he wanted to surprise him, but he must have phoned ahead because Abu Ben was waiting on the steps with an expectant expression on his face.

It changed to pure joy when Shane

stepped out with the now-sleeping child.

The sheik could not stem the flood of tears that threatened to drown him. Romy had to turn aside, the show of emotion was too strong to bear. Shane took her hand as they waited for the sheik to compose himself.

Presently they all went indoors and Tanita was taken away to be fed and bathed. Afterwards the sheik wanted to know exactly what had happened.

They talked until the dawn and drank endless cups of coffee till Romy, who had been yawning for the past hour, said she really had to go back to the hotel and get to bed.

"But won't you stay here?" suggested the sheik. "I would be greatly honoured if you could see your way to staying."

They started to protest but the sheik insisted they must stay the night at the palace as he had already arranged for rooms to be made available for them

After that it seemed churlish not to accept his hospitality.

Romy's room which was light and airy with a high ceiling, was furnished in Eastern style with native mats on the floor and pottery pieces depicting scenes from Egypt's colourful past. On the flocked wallpaper were papyrus pictures of old Egypt with camels and pyramids. From outside the windows came the smell of exotic flowers and she was quite drugged by their perfume. However, much she would have liked to explore she admitted to being too tired.

The great bed beckoned and she succumbed to it. She was asleep the moment her head touched the fragrant pillows.

The next thing she knew was Shane's voice outside on the communal balcony. He peeped his head round the gold brocade curtain. "Come on, sleepy-head. I've been up for hours."

"Shut up and go away!" she mumbled irritably.

"My word, you're grumpy." He took a pace into the room. "You should get up and do some exercises. It'll set you up for the day."

"Shut up and go away! Why is early rising considered a virtue?"

"I didn't imagine you were bad-tempered in the morning." He went to the windows and threw back the curtains.

She blinked at the sudden brightness. "I don't want those undrawn."

"And to think I asked you to marry me," he went on relentlessly. "I've had a narrow escape to be sure."

She threw a pillow at him and he ducked out to the balcony again.

There came a tap on the door and a young Arab maid entered bearing a loaded breakfast tray. She gave Romy a wide smile and waited till she had struggled into a sitting position then placed the tray on her knees. She plumped up the pillows and went to the windows but seeing the curtains were already undrawn threw Romy another smile, opened the door and went out.

Romy thanked her as she withdrew.

Romy looked with delight at the little pots of preserve, the hot croissants and the pats of butter There was a jug of coffee, cream and sugar and a freshly plucked rose in a slim vase.

She couldn't believe how hungry she was and wondered what the time was. A glance at her watch made her jump into action. It was noon. Whatever would Alex say?

She simply had to take a bath and sped across the room to the en suite bathroom. She gasped in wonder at the enchanting sight that met her eyes. There was a sunken gold bath and the tiles on the walls depicted a scene of life-sized dolphins leaping from the sea. A splendid array of expensive toiletries was on the shelves. The towels were lavender with gold motifs of an eagle. She surmised that this was the sheik's crest because she recalled having seen it on several items before.

She couldn't have hurried if she had been paid to. After she had added to the bath a generous amount of ylang-ylang bubble oil she sank gratefully into the hot water and wallowed.

When she finally dressed in the spice-coloured linen dress she had put on — was it only yesterday? — and dragged a comb through her tangled locks, she descended the ornate staircase.

Shane was waiting at the foot looking slightly agitated. "We'll have missed the morning's filming," he said as if he blamed her. "I've never been late on set before."

Before she could defend herself, the sheik approached hand in hand with Tanita.

"Ah, there you are, Romy," he bellowed, "We want to thank you for all you did . . . "

"No time," she cut in. "Alex will go spare if we don't put in an appearance soon."

"It's okay, I've spoken to your director and put things all right." The sheik gave a little bow. "I am in your debt. Ask for anything you want and it is yours."

Romy was taken aback at his generosity. "All I want is for the filming to be completed with no more delays," she said.

"Yes," agreed Shane, "That would be something else. Think you can fix it, sheik?"

"Sorry." He looked forlorn. "I meant some jewellery. Or some bloodstock."

They declined his offer and he put his Rolls at their disposal.

They drove back to their hotel in style.

"You know everyone bows to a Rolls," mused Shane. "You give it room on the road and you don't mind it passing you. Usually it means someone has done well for himself and, even if he was born to it, it shows he has good taste."

"Yes, I suppose you're right," she murmured, caressing the white leather of the seat. "I've never looked at it like that before."

* * *

The papers that evening were full of their exploits and Romy was cheered as she entered the restaurant.

She also learned that three of the Falcon gang had been captured the previous afternoon and were safely behind bars.

"That's a relief," she told Martin. "I hope that's the lot of them. I suppose you can never be certain."

He held the chair for her but before she could sit down she was wanted on the phone. It was the sheik asking if she had heard the news and informing her that when the kidnappers had been picked up at the airport they had the diamonds intact.

She passed this news on to Shane who had joined them at the table.

Martin looked peeved. "You two are the toast of the town." He continued in a grumbling way. "I wish it had been me instead of Shane who did all that derring do. I thought I was the brave one around here but you showed your mettle, Shane. I shall have to see what I can do to get myself into Romy's good books again."

Romy slid into the seat. "Don't be silly, Martin. You don't have to prove anything to me."

His spirits visibly lifted whilst Shane's sank.

After dinner Alex caught up with Romy on the stairs.

"Well, well," he said in a supercilious tone of voice. "I didn't know I had such famous people working for me. I shall have to watch myself. No doubt you will find it quite boring working on the commercial now. However we've got to finish it and I should be grateful if you could give it your special attention from now on."

Romy felt chastened. "I'm sorry, Alex, I really am. It's too bad of me to have let you down like that. I'm well aware you can't function without a make-up girl."

"It's not only that." He took her arm

and they continued up the stairs. "It was a very dangerous thing to do. How do you think I felt waiting for news? It was hell! You might have been killed! For God's sake, Romy, what did you think you were doing?"

"I've said I'm sorry." She was at a loss to know what else she could do.

"You put me through torture, do you know that? I love you, Romy."

He tried to take her in his arms, but she was too quick for him.

She ran away from him and locked herself in her room.

6

IT came hard getting back in the old routine after what she had been through but Romy knuckled down to it. The money for the extras had now arrived and there was nothing to stop them going ahead.

As Romy made up Shane's face she mused that here was a man who she'd thought she had known but he was more complex of character than she had imagined possible. He wasn't at all the stereotyped male model and she viewed him now with some trepidation. She recalled his proposal of marriage and how she had laughed in his face. It was quite unnerving to be working on him. She was unable to meet his gaze for most of the time and was aware that his breathing had quickened the moment he took the chair.

It really was a physical thing they

shared and she fell to daydreaming, wondering what it would be like being his lover. She recalled that look they had exchanged just before she had driven off with the diamonds, when she had been filled with desire for him. It hardly made sense. She didn't like him, not in that way, Was she falling under that mythical spell he was supposed to possess? No? that was impossible. Her thoughts were making her dizzy.

At midday the sheik arrived with presents for everyone. Romy received a magnificent bolt of silk, enough to make at least six suits. It was a subtle shade of damson. She would be able to give some of it to her mother.

They continued with the commercial and everything seemed to be plain sailing at last. The extras, now with money in their pockets, were eager to please. Romy watched them practising their movements. It was then she noticed that one of them, a small timid-looking man, was staring at her in a curious way. She hadn't seen him before and wondered if he was one of the regular extras.

She swallowed hard. Somehow he made her feel threatened. Was he in any way connected with the kidnappers? From the little hair she could see above his burnous, he was redheaded. Was he related to the woman, Stefana? She was sure they had no redheaded extras — it wouldn't look authentic. Not that she hadn't seen plenty of red-haired Arabs but people expected them to be dark.

Fear ran through her as she remembered the woman's words concerning what she would like to do to Romy given half a chance. "I'd make her wish she'd never been born." The Spanish were noted for their family pride and a brother could be seeking revenge.

She felt the hairs on the back of her neck tingling and returned to her tent.

When Decima came in after her final scene Romy asked her if she had noticed the little extra.

"I haven't got time to bother with

extras," she said haughtily. "All my energy goes on getting out of the way of those camels."

Romy chewed her lip. She could have been mistaken. But she had a premonition that she had not heard the last of the affair. She sought Martin out during the lunch break and asked him his opinion.

He hadn't noticed anyone who shouldn't have been there. He thought she was over-reacting, he said. "You've had one adventure and you don't want to return to the real world."

"You're a great help," she grumbled at him. "I'm about to be murdered and you think I'm over-reacting."

"Look, Romy, if you feel this man is a threat you must go to the police."

"Yes, you're another one. If the sheik had gone to the police he might never have seen his daughter again."

"I'm afraid you've lost me," he said scratching his head.

She was beginning to think there was something in the saying 'all brawn and no brain' after all.

After the filming had finished for that day, the crew made their way to an open-air theatre where a *Son et Lumière* was taking place. Alex was treating them all to the spectacle.

As they entered the auditorium he lightly took Romy's arm and guided her to a seat beside him. She had no option but to remain there. She saw both Martin and Shane looking put out. She smiled at them and gave a little shrug.

She put her bag on the floor and leaned back in the seat to enjoy herself. The laser beams were dazzlingly dramatic and the spectacle was a magnificent feast for the eyes. It featured historical events followed by their modern-day counterparts, such as the building of the pyramids and the Suez canal.

During the interval Alex took Romy to the bar and no sooner had he got her a gin and tonic than she was jostled and she spilt it all down her new chiffon dress. It was the colour of ripe apricots and she loved it. She turned angrily to the person who had bumped into her and found herself staring into the face of the same extra who had caused her so much anguish that afternoon. She stood there gaping, trying to put things into perspective. This wasn't the man, he was far too thin. She sighed with relief and admonished herself for letting it get on her nerves.

She told Alex she wanted to call it a day as the show came to an end, pleading a headache. It was plain he did not believe her but that was his problem she figured. He took her back to the hotel and insisted on buying her a drink. His speech was slightly slurred and she hazarded a guess that he'd been drinking before they met.

"Go on, it'll do you good." He smiled sympathetically. "Your head will clear in no time."

She shrugged her acquiesence and chose a table under the lights.

He laughed wryly. "You don't trust

me one little bit, do you?"

Oh dear, was it so obvious?

She drained her vodka and tonic in one gulp and stood up. "Well, goodnight Alex, it's been nice."

He trailed after her to her door. As she put her key in the lock he sprang towards her almost sending her flying.

He stopped her from falling by pulling her into his arms. His mouth sought hers and she was under that old spell again. But not for long. She actually felt some disgust for his spirit laden breath.

"Please don't," she said tensely. "I really do have the most awful headache."

He took no notice.

As he came in for a second kiss she kicked out at him. She caught him on the shin and he gasped with pain and let her go. She took advantage of his preoccupation and sped away into her room. It was a yale lock so she only had to push the door to and she was safe.

"You little bitch," he snarled through

the door. “You lead me on then you run away. There’s a name for women like you.”

She bit her lip in agitation.

“You think you’re in love with Shane Shelley, don’t you?” he shouted. “Well he won’t be any good to you. He’s a ‘here-today-gone-tomorrow’ kind of guy.”

She didn’t bother to reply.

“What is he? Nothing but a pretty face. Take that away and what have you got?” He sounded thoughtful for a moment. “Yes, take the pretty face away and . . . ”

She crossed the bedroom to switch on the radio and turn the volume up.

He called out a few more insults then she heard him move away bumping into the hall furniture as he went.

She wondered what she had ever seen in him. He had been her star ascendant on the horizon of her dreams. She had been unable to see any future without him. Now suddenly the future looked rosy. She was over him! Over Alex!

She sat down on the bed, feeling lightheaded as the message sank in. It was as if a giant weight had been lifted from her shoulders. Oh it felt good! She wanted to tell someone and Shane came to mind. That was strange because it was Martin whom she fancied. It must be because of what Alex had just said. Oh boy! Had he got the wrong end of the stick. Still he could think what he liked.

It wasn't till she had climbed into bed that it occurred to her to question why Alex had thought she was in love with Shane. She had always thought him such a good judge of character, it sort of went with the job. But she had to admit he wasn't in the best state to judge anything when he suggested that.

She snuggled down and grinned at the ceiling before all her reasoning was postponed till morning.

* * *

They were coming to the end of the commercial. It had taken a week longer than anticipated thanks to the camels, the extras and the kidnappers.

Romy wasn't wanted on the set that morning because they were looking at the rushes — the scenes they had so far in the can. She decided to wash some smalls and was busy at the wash basin in her room when there came a light tap on the door.

She dried her hands and went to answer it.

She recoiled in alarm for there stood the skinny ginger-haired man she had thought was Stefana's brother. He wore western dress, not too clean, and a cheroot dangled from his slack mouth.

He forced himself into the room, pushing her in front of him and kicked the door shut.

In fractured English he said, "Making no noise or . . . " And he did a mime of someone having their throat cut.

She ran to the phone but before she could pick up the receiver he leapt in front of her and ripped it from the wall.

She picked up the jug of bottled water remembering how she had used a jug as a weapon before. But it wasn't going to work this time because he wrenched it from her and slung it across the room drenching the duvet.

"Who are you?" she demanded. "You have no right . . . "

He lashed out at her face with the back of his hand but she saw it coming and took evasive action. As she dodged away the blow caught her shoulder. It hurt. Her assailant may be painfully thin but he was strong.

There came another knock on the door and she sighed with relief. "Help!" she called, rubbing her shoulder, "There's a maniac in here . . . "

To her surprise the man opened the door and welcomed in another man, this time a well-dressed executive type, even handsome with his chin cleanshaven and the smell of Brute emanating from his person to fill the room with its unmistakable fragrance.

"I'm glad you've come, Lord Henry. She's a tiger."

Lord? thought Romy, thoroughly confused.

"Ricardo, what are you up to?" the newcomer asked languidly perfect English. In fact it was so perfect that Romy took him to be English.

Ricardo gave a loose continental shrug which emphasized his skinny frame. "She was going for the phone . . . "

"That's no excuse for hitting a lady."

Lord Henry, if that was his name, came to stand in front of Romy. He put out a hand to the shoulder that she was still rubbing. "There there," he crooned.

Romy didn't know what to make of him.

Turning to Ricardo he said in a voice that was loaded with sexual overtones, "There are more ways to skin a cat than . . . " And he touched the side of his nose and winked.

Romy shuddered. She thought she'd rather take her chances with the ruffian.

The second man's attention returned to her. "And she is so pretty. It would be sacrilege to hurt her. Yet."

Romy thought rapidly but there was nothing she could do. The crew were all watching the rushes. The chambermaids had been and gone. She was going to be molested by this 'lord' and there wasn't a thing she could do about it. She looked at the carpet and offered up a silent prayer.

She heard the door open and raised her head. Lord Henry was poking his head out, looking up and down the corridor.

Before she knew what was happening Ricardo had hold of her arms and was frog-marching her across the room.

"Right, it's all clear. Quickly!" said Lord Henry. "Now!"

As Ricardo pushed her into the corridor, she opened her mouth to scream. He immediately clamped his hand over her mouth. It smelt like old tennis shoes and she was very nearly sick.

"One sound from you and it's curtains," said Lord Henry over his shoulder.

She was led to a flight of narrow stairs, leading to the servants' quarters by the quality of the carpet. Up and up they went, along passageways and more stairs until they reached what Romy felt had to be the attic area.

Ricardo opened a door and she was thrust in. He locked the door behind them.

It was then Romy noticed a woman sitting in a rocking chair, in a pool of light from the overhead fanlight. She gasped out loud. It was Stefana!

"How did . . . I thought you were in jail."

"I am Nestafa. My *sister* Stefana is in jail thanks to you."

Romy looked again. This woman had red hair but she was younger than Stefana, in fact not much older than Romy.

"Bring her here under the light," she ordered. When they had done so she peered hard into Romy's face. "Skinny little thing." She spoke good English, hardly accented at all. "And rather insipid." She touched Romy's long blonde hair. "I don't know what the world's coming to if a weakling like this can overthrow the likes of the Falcon."

"Now look here," said Romy briskly. "I don't know what you want with me, but I warn you I am a British citizen and I have rights . . . "

The woman had opened her eyes wide and now she narrowed them and burst out laughing. The men joined in. It was a horrid sound and made Romy shiver. She shook Ricardo's staying hand away and marched forthrightly towards the door.

Lord Henry barred her way. "And where do you think you're going?"

She made to push past him but he

caught her arms and pinioned them to her sides.

She could feel the strength in him, the sheer brute force of his muscles. It terrified her. No way could she talk herself out of this. He had brawn and, intelligence too, she wouldn't be surprised to discover. He looked the public school type. He may be dressed in a casual fashion but his simple tee-shirt and jeans screamed Savile Row. She decided to bluff her way out of this situation.

"Kindly let me pass," she said frostily. "I'm needed on the set."

The woman had been rocking away in the chair but now she stood up. "Enough of this arguing. Take the girl to the Round House."

Ricardo sprang into action, seizing Romy around the waist and throwing her over his shoulder.

She screamed and he hissed, "Do again and I tape your mouth."

She was carried out of the room and down the same back stairs. Then out into the open to a kind of walled courtyard. They met no-one and Romy despaired. She was bundled into the back of a car and Ricardo got in after her.

Nestafa got into the driver's seat and was joined by Lord Henry.

"Where are you taking me?" Romy asked as they drove off

Nestafa's eyes met hers in the rear-view mirror. "Where your screams can't be heard."

Romy swallowed hard. Was she joking? She didn't look the type of woman who would joke. In fact she had the sort of face that would crack if she laughed.

Lord Henry said, "You promised me you'd let me have her first." He sounded peeved.

"I've changed my mind," snapped Nestafa. "My sister is very religious. She wouldn't be pleased if you assaulted this girl in the name of revenge."

Henry scowled. "You might have told me that before you let me lend you that thousand pounds."

"You'll get it back."

"That's not the point. I demand you give it back to me now."

"That will be a little difficult. You know we've spent it."

"Then you must keep to your side of the bargain."

"Very well." Nestafa clamped her lips tightly together. "You may have her for half an hour."

"It's enough."

Romy had been listening to the conversation with alarm. They were arguing over who should vent their spleen on her first. Whoever won the consequences didn't look too good. She could guess what form the punishment would take where Lord Henry was concerned, but from what she had heard the woman's revenge for her sister would leave her dead.

Nestafa was no better a driver than her sister and Romy soon began to feel sick from the jolting. She came to dread corners where she was thrown about like an empty box.

After they had covered some miles Nestafa ordered Lord Henry to blindfold Romy and she reckoned they were getting near to their destination.

When they had driven for an hour at least Romy thought they must have reached the outskirts of the city. The woman slowed down and as the car stopped the blindfold was removed.

Romy saw they were in a dark courtyard of what looked like an old fortress. She could understand why they called it the Round House for it appeared to be a circular building.

Nestafa got out and stood rubbing her back. "The others are late," she said, staring along the road. "They should have been here to meet us."

Romy was hauled out of the car by Henry who pulled her roughly towards the massive door.

"Half an hour, mind," said Nestafa in a surly voice.

"Don't worry."

"I don't know why you want to mess

around with her. She's too skinny and she looks frigid."

He leered. "Just the way I like them."

Henry had unlocked the door by inserting a great iron key in the lock and now he pushed at the door with all his strength. It opened slowly and he dragged her inside.

They were in a vast chamber rather like a Scottish baronial hall. It was devoid of all furniture and there was a thick layer of dust over the floor which set Romy sneezing.

Henry locked the door behind them and stood looking about him. It was gloomy, the only light coming from a window high above them in the domed roof.

"If you let me go," said Romy, "My parents will be pleased to pay you any ransom you care to name — within reason." She saw him watching her closely. "Here, take this." She took off her watch. "It's an expensive one, to show my good intent. I promise not to go to the police."

He grinned. "It's okay. I'm not going to harm you."

She was confused. Where had the public school accent gone?

"I don't understand."

"It's all right, darling, I'm not a rapist. I'm just someone working for British Customs and Excise."

She still couldn't grasp what he was talking about, and she felt faint. There was nowhere to sit and she swayed about dizzily.

His arms came out to save her and he held her to his chest till she stopped trembling.

"There, if you feel you can stand up, I'll go and see if I can find something to sit on."

"Yes. yes, I can stand. But will you please tell me what's going on."

"All in good time," he replied as he went over to a second door.

She felt lightheaded. A moment before she was going to be violated and now she wasn't. It was as simple as that. She couldn't begin to think what was going on, she only knew she had an ally in Lord Henry.

He returned, carrying a dusty spindly-legged chair and set it down in front of her. Then took out an immaculate white handkerchief and dusted the seat. "There you go."

She flopped down gratefully. "Are you really a lord?"

"Hell, no!"

"Then what are you?"

He perched on the slim edge of the window sill. "It's a long and complicated story. The gist of it is that I'm on undercover work. We've been watching the Falcon gang for several months now. They're only small-time terrorists but they create a lot of aggro. While I had Ricardo under surveillance I overheard him discussing someone who they were going to kidnap and torture and eventually kill. You."

Romy gasped. "Oh my God!"

"I managed to find out who they were talking about — a girl on the film set, the one who did the make-up — and knew I had to stop them."

Romy got up from the chair. "I see, so then you turned yourself into Lord Henry."

"Yes, I was brilliant, wasn't I?"

"Well, you certainly fooled me."

"I found out they were short of a thousand pounds for some project they were working on, so I posed as a member of the British aristocracy. A decadent member of the aristocracy. I agreed to lend them a thousand in return for some very depraved favours."

He left the window ledge. "I'm sorry I couldn't let you in on the secret. But you might have given the game away if you weren't scared enough."

"I see but I wish you could have told me. I was absolutely terrified."

"Well, you're all right now. And you mustn't waste any more time. How are you at running?"

R . . . Running?"

"Hold on! I'd better call up my colleagues first. They're staked out down the road and are waiting for my call. The rest of the gang will be here shortly. All seven of them. I can't handle them on my own." He took out a mobile phone. "I'll want some back-up for when they find out you've escaped."

He got through and seemed to be talking in code for she could understand not one word.

"That's settled." He pushed the aerial down and pocketed the handset. "Listen, I'll tell you what to do."

"I wish you would."

"Here." He scooped up a handful of dust. "Rub this on your face. We're in a poor area and you look too clean."

She did as he suggested. She was already dirty so what did a little more matter?

He grinned and his teeth flashed white in his own dirty face. "You look a sight."

"Hark who's talking!"

He went to the farther door and opened it.

"I noticed when I went for the chair that there was a back entrance. I only hope those two don't know about it."

A large and rusty key was hanging on a hook beside the door. Henry tried it in the lock but it wouldn't turn. Romy thought she might die from frustration.

"What now?" she asked dejectedly.

"Don't despair. I think the whole door is rotten. It shouldn't take much to smash it down." He took a running jump at it and crashed into it with both feet. The door shook violently and one panel dropped out.

"Hell!" he said. "That was some noise. I hope they didn't hear it." He stood silently for a moment, his head cocked at a listening angle. "No, it's okay."

He put his hand through the hole in the door and took out the surrounding panels till there was room for them to climb through.

She peered about, blinking in the sudden sunshine after the gloom of the Round House. There was a gate in a wall and it opened quite easily.

"You're to go as fast as you can without actually running . . . "

"I thought you said I'd got to run."

"Run in the sense of running away," he corrected her. "If you run you'll draw attention to yourself. This is a dangerous area especially for a young woman on her own."

She felt an icy finger of fear climb her backbone. "Thanks for telling me."

"Ah, forewarned is forearmed." He took her elbow. "I wish I could accompany you, but I have crispier fish to fry."

She thought he was one for cliches.

He pointed. "Down there is a labyrinth of alleyways. You must not linger there . . . "

"Don't you worry!"

"There is a lane that will take you to the main road where you can get a taxi. It's called the Street of Weeping Women."

"Hm! Sounds ominous."

He watched her anxiously. “Are you going to be all right?” He looked guilty. “Only I’d hate to miss this round-up.”

She gulped. “I’m okay.”

There came the sound in the distance of powerful cars heading their way. “That’ll be the rest of the gang. I only hope my colleagues are on the way behind them,” he said. “Or this could end up very nastily for me.”

He patted her shoulder then thrust her out into the street. She heard the door shut behind her. She was on her own. She realised she hadn’t thanked him. She regretted that in immensely. For he had undoubtedly saved her life.

She was glad therefore when she saw two cars heading in the direction of the Round House, sirens blaring.

There were lanes leading in all directions. And none of them called The Street of Weeping Women.

She decided to take the centre one and strode briskly along it. There were no people here and she wondered if Henry had deliberately tried to frighten her.

The lane was lined with tumbledown warehouses, seemingly deserted and she was almost at the end of it when a crowd of men came round the corner.

They stopped and stared. For a whole minute there was utter silence. Then Bedlam broke out. They all started shouting at once as they circled her. They were all ages, young boys barely old enough to shave, middle-aged men with flowing moustaches and old grandfather types.

One of the latter began stroking her hair. She tried to pull it from his grasp but only succeeded in leaving golden strands in his hand.

He smiled and held it aloft as if it were a scalp.

The others, not to be outdone, gathered around and started pulling her hair out by the roots.

She screamed and ran for all she was worth. Hurtling round the first corner she came to a doorway and took refuge inside what looked like a factory. It was deserted but there was evidence of recent occupation by a fire burning low in the grate. She crept stealthily to a further door from whence came the sound of voices. Peering round she saw three women with their backs to her. They were working on some kind of tapestry which looked complicated.

She glanced behind her to make sure she wasn't being followed then ran past the startled women and out by another exit.

Romy saw she was on the edge of a market. She could smell coffee and spices and see the sun sparkling on some fine glass. There were brightly-coloured stalls piled high with fruit and vegetables, most of them strange to her, And some wonderful carpets were displayed outside a big warehouse.

She felt confident to find a way out of this maze and walked on, straight into the arms of a very tall man.

7

THE man was winded and doubled over to get his breath. She took this opportunity to attempt to escape but he shot out a hand to stop her.

"Let me go," she shrieked. "Why don't you keep your hands to yourself."

The man was dressed in a flowing burnous and he looked very fierce but she wasn't afraid of him. She had too many things on her mind and fear of one more man had to go to the back of the queue.

He stared down at her from his great height. "What have we got here?" He spoke in Arabic first then in good English.

She wriggled frantically to be free of him but was no match for his strength.

"You little wild thing. I'm not going to harm you."

She gave an almighty wriggle and broke free. As quickly as she could she dodged into another open doorway.

She was in a primitive kitchen where several woman were cooking a meal. They stopped what they were doing and watched her with weary eyes.

She gave a helpless shrug and continued past them into a back room which was empty except for a large cupboard. She tried the door and found it was also empty. She squeezed into it and pulled the door to.

There came a noise of shouting and she heard the tall man speaking to the women. She didn't hear their reply.

She discovered a knothole and through it saw him come into the room. He stopped in front of the cupboard but didn't seem to notice it. She wondered how long she could hold her breath.

After a few moments he went through yet another door. She could hear him talking to someone and their muffled reply.

She strained her ears and heard

the voices growing more distant as if the person he had spoken with was accompanying him in the search.

She waited another moment and then came warily out of the cupboard and flew back the way she had come. The women took no notice of her this time.

No sooner had she left the building than she heard footsteps behind her and realised the tall man was on her trail again. She rushed down the nearest alleyway — and came to a dead end.

"Come here!" he shouted. "I'm not going to hurt you."

Jack the Ripper probably said that to his victims she thought as she turned to face him. "Leave me alone!" she cried. "I don't know what's the matter with you Egyptian men. One sight of a woman and you lose your rag."

"Will you shut up and listen to me." He stood there arms akimbo in a menacing attitude. "I want the reward for finding you, that's all."

"What . . . what did you say?" She

felt ready to faint and thought she might be hallucinating.

"You heard!"

"Look! Will you tell me what you're going on about," she cried with exasperation. "I shall have a coronary if I don't find out soon what's happening."

"Talkative little baggage, aren't you? It's quite simple. The local radio station announced you were missing and that there was a reward. I recognise you from the description. Blonde hair, petite, pretty, very English looking." He came nearer and held out a hand. "Come with me and I'll take you to the police station."

She looked at him, her head on one side, and tried to gauge if he was genuine. She decided that sooner or later she had got to trust someone.

"Thanks," she said, hoping he wasn't a white slaver.

The group of men she had encountered earlier came charging round the corner and stopped in their tracks.

Their eyes lit up at the sight of Romy.

The tall man said something to them and they scowled at him but kept coming.

He began to shout at them and shook his fists. They seemed very much afraid of him and reluctantly drifted away. When they were a safe distance away they turned and hurled abuse at him. He ignored them.

"Thanks," she said again.

"Thanks are not needed," he said, "I did it for the reward." He opened the door of an old banger of a car standing nearby and indicated she should get in.

As she hesitated he gave her a push an she fell into the front passenger seat.

He climbed in beside her and there began the most nerve-wracking drive she had ever undertaken. He had no brakes and travelled on both sides of the road in turn. She felt as if she were in a dodgem car at the fair and, looking down, could see the road through great holes in the floor.

She was thankful when they reached the police station and she was still all in one piece.

There were a few formalities to deal with then Romy was on her way. She said goodbye to her tall saviour and said she hoped he would get the reward money all right.

"What's your name?" she asked.

He looked cagey for a moment and then said, "No purpose will be served by you knowing my name."

She was disappointed but accepted that he was probably a crook living on his wits.

The man at the desk said they would run her home in a police car and it took her directly to the hotel.

Martin was on the forecourt looking out for her. He bounded forward like dog at the sight of his master. "Thank goodness you've been found. When the police phoned just now with the news that you were okay I was so happy I could have wept with joy."

She was taken aback by what was for

him a long speech and the message it contained. He really had missed her!

He seized her in his arms and kissed her there in front of the people passing by.

"Why Martin," she gasped, conscious that his kiss had done nothing for her. "I didn't think you were one for public displays."

A sheepish look befell him and he glanced furtively over his shoulder before letting her go. "Forgive me, Romy, I don't know what came over me."

"Oh, don't apologise. I enjoyed it," she lied.

"Did you. Romy, did you really?"

"Stop putting yourself down," she told him. "You're a nice man."

He grinned broadly and putting his arm around her guided her into the hotel lounge

The whole crew was there and they rose as Romy entered. A cheer went up and she blushed.

Alex took her arm in such a

masterful way that Martin was forced to relinquish his hold.

"Glad to see you back, Romy, my dear," he said quietly. "I've been out of my mind with worry."

She forced a smile.

Shane came up to her next and, ignoring Alex's hand, pressed his lips to her cheek. "Welcome home," he murmured.

Alex looked fiercely at Shane and said, "Is there something going on between you two?"

Romy opened her mouth to deny it but before she could speak Shane said, "What if there is?"

She could have killed him.

"What did you have to say that for?" she asked him when Alex had gone to the bar.

"Because it's true," he said complacently. "And the sooner he gets that into his thick head the better."

"Oh, there's no talking to you." And she flounced off to her room for a long-overdue bath.

As she lay in the fragrant water she went over the events of the day. Safe in the confines of the hotel she could hardly credit what had taken place. It was all too far-fetched by half. Had she really been kidnapped, taken to the Round House, set free by a man called Lord Henry, run away along those twisting lanes and met a tall man?

She had some time to spare before supper so wrote another letter to her brother beginning.

'You're never going to believe what's happened to me since I last wrote.'

That evening they heard on the radio that the notorious Falcon gang which had been terrorising the people of Cairo for months had finally been captured and would probably be deported back to Spain.

Romy went down to supper with Martin and Shane.

"We've decided you can't be trusted to be let out on your own," said Shane with a wink at Martin, "so we're forming your body-guard."

"What a cheek!" said Romy, "It's not me, it's those Spaniards."

"You seem to attract trouble," Martin added. "It's for your own good."

"That's what my mum used to say when she wanted to give me nasty medicine."

There was a dance at the hotel at ten o'clock and the three of them went along to the ballroom. The band was local but the music was universal. 'Moon River' was being played as they entered and Shane immediately grabbed Romy and pulled her onto the dance-floor.

"How are you with the foxtrot?"

"Not too bad," she murmured, going into his arms.

She glanced over his shoulder at Martin standing all alone and tried to catch his eye to give him a smile that would show him she would rather be dancing with him. But he was staring intently at the carpet. She would have to get rid of Shane somehow.

He was a marvellous dancer she discovered and very easy to follow. All she had to do was keep in step. His grip was very sensual and he used all of his body while his chin was pressed to her temple. Despite their closeness he still managed to dip her most professionally. She was feeling quite flustered by the time the dance ended and he had pulled her arm through his and escorted her back to their table.

She took Martin's arm and said brightly, "Will you dance the next one with me?"

Martin looked hang-dogged. "I'm sorry but I can't dance."

She didn't know what to say next.

Shane said, "Do you want to do this tango with me?"

The tango was her favourite dance but she declined his offer because of Martin. She couldn't bear to see him so miserable.

Shane went and asked Decima to dance.

"Would you like to sit outside?" Martin offered.

She jumped at the chance. Shane wouldn't follow them, she felt sure. He was too much of a gentleman to play gooseberry. The moment this thought occurred to her she wondered how she came to that conclusion. She didn't really know the man. Then why did she feel so sure?

Martin fetched some drinks and they found a bench under the sweet-smelling trees.

"What are you thinking about?"

"Sh . . . " She stopped. It wasn't very complimentary to talk about his rival. "Shopping" she finished lamely.

By the look on his face he wasn't fooled. "If you want to go shopping I'll take you."

"Oh will you, Martin, I would be grateful."

She wondered what was the matter with her. She was behaving so out of character. She didn't usually have to resort to lying to boyfriends.

* * *

"So you really think there's nothing going on between us?"

Romy and Shane were sitting drinking coffee under the gaudy flame trees in the hotel garden.

She gave a nervous laugh and studied him through her downcast lashes.

He shot out of his seat to embrace her so suddenly that he almost sent her chair flying. "Romy, my darling. I love you and I think you love me . . . " His words were muffled against her mouth.

Could it be true?

"Romy! You are an idiot. Why won't you admit you can't get enough of me?"

His lips came towards her again and now his kiss seemed to worship her mouth. Her lungs were bursting for air by the time he had finished. His next kiss had her clinging to him as if her very existence depended upon it.

He said: "There! Now do you believe me?"

He had her seriously worried now. Could it have been Shane all along?

No! She refused to accept it. After Alex, she'd valued her freedom and meant never again to rely on a man for her happiness. Women had come a long way since Mrs Pankhurst and it was up to her not to let the side down.

She admitted to herself she had only been playing with Martin. It was probably the fact that he was unlikely to declare himself that had attracted him to her in the first place.

Sharon, the odd-job girl, came out into the garden and said: "Oh Shane, Alex's looking for you. He wants to shoot one of your scenes again."

"Rightio," said Shane. "You'd better come too, Romy."

He took out his mobile phone to get in touch with Alex while Romy raced upstairs for her make-up bag.

Shane said as they sped across the

city in a taxi: "Alex's going to let me do one of my own stunts. He knows how keen I am. Not a word to Martin."

"Oh, no!" exclaimed Romy aghast. "Which scene is it?"

"The-death-defying-jump-over-the-canyon scene."

"Oh no!" she cried again, staring at him in horror. "That's much too dangerous. What can Alex be thinking of?"

"I was only kidding," he confessed. "Actually I'm doing the jumping-onto-a-horse-and-riding-into-town scene."

She gave a heartfelt sigh. "Thank goodness! I wish you wouldn't frighten me like that," she exploded. Then she added, "It's a bit better — but not much."

"He knows I want to do my own stunts eventually and he's generously giving me a practice."

"You should start with something easier."

"Alex assured me it is easy. Much easier than it looks."

Presently, she was installed in the tent working on Shane's face. That dear face of the man she loved

"Do you honestly think you can do it?" she asked preparing a clean brush.

"Just jumping on a horse? You've got to be joking! Who rescued you from death in the desert? Who brought you home on his horse?"

She held up her hands in surrender. "Okay, Okay! So you can ride a horse."

He stood up and beamed at her. "O ye of little faith. Trust me, Romy, my love. You've seen me in action, breaking down that door and toppling those two crooks with a fender." He jutted his chin and effected an heroic pose. "I was quite impressive, wasn't I?"

"There you go, boasting again." She wrung out the face cloth. "But I must admit you were impressive."

"Thank you." He spoke in a sing-song sarcastic kind of way. "Well, are you going to let me do this little thing?"

"I suppose so," she pouted. "But be careful."

"Trust me. Prudent is my middle name." He watched her for some time, head on one side then said, "Gimme a good luck kiss then."

He lifted her from the floor and into his arms. His kiss when it came was hard but she matched it and the heady feeling of belonging was as intoxicating as wine.

Slowly his mouth slid over hers in an almost aggressive way. She was aware of the slight stubble she had been ordered to keep on. Time seemed of no account as they remained lost in that fond embrace. Eventually his lips drew away and they gazed at each other.

In Romy's head there formed a memory of Alex saying something about Shane being only a pretty face and what use would he be without it.

Alex wouldn't, would he? He wouldn't let Shane do a difficult stunt that might leave him disfigured? Not in front of the camera crew? But he was terribly jealous, and he seemed certain she had fallen for the handsome model.

No. She couldn't accept that Alex would be so vindictive. And yet, from the way he had treated her, she knew he was capable of anything — and her blood turned to ice.

Shane was saying: "You were sensational yesterday. But I can't understand how you took so long to discover you wanted me."

Before she could reply they heard Alex outside. "Are you going to be much longer?" he asked irritably.

Shane threw aside the smock and gave Romy another, brief, kiss. "Just coming," he called.

He gave her a look that could only be described as a smirk. "I will return to you, my darling, I promise. And all in one piece. And then we'll carry on where we left off."

They heard someone cough in the tent entrance as Shane lowered her to floor. They both swung round to see

Alex, barely hiding his anger.

Before either of them could speak he turned on his heel and left the tent.

Romy silently prayed that he would not take his anger out on Shane.

They went outside to where Alex was waiting. The two men went off in the direction of the cameras and Romy stayed where she was.

Lost in thought, she went over in her mind all that was bothering her. The make-up job she had been asked to do was indeed for the jump-on-the-horse scene, but it would also do for the dangerous canyon scene. She supposed she was being ridiculous thinking Alex would deliberately try to ruin Shane's looks. Just because he was jealous of him over her, Romy. That was vanity pure and simple. It was a wonder her turban hat fitted her!

The clapper-board boy came over to tell her she wasn't needed any more and could go.

Why? she wondered, So she wasn't a witness to what was about to happen?

Normally when she was dismissed early she was pleased. She didn't think anyone was going to be killed. She tried to put things into perspective and went to look for a cab. But the suspicions lingered. Would Alex have the nerve? No, the cameramen were there. She was being ridiculous.

Martin was in the lounge with Decima and a few others and he passed on to her the sheik's invitation to join him on a trip to Alexandria in one of his private planes.

"One of them!" she exclaimed.

"That's what the man said."

She put her worries about Alex's filming firmly behind her and said she'd love to come.

"Won't be a moment. I'll just pop upstairs and put on something sensational."

She put on a two-piece in ice-blue cotton over a white camisole. It was the only outfit she had with a top designer label in it and she had been keeping it for the last evening when they usually celebrated in style.

She considered this warranted something special.

The sheik himself took the controls and he had brought Tanita along.

The plane was large by usual standards and those of the crew who were not engaged on the final rework, all managed to get in quite comfortably. Abu Ben patted the seat beside him and Romy slid into it. At once Martin took the seat next to her.

She felt hemmed in.

It seemed strange that she should feel like that. Hadn't she been trying to get Martin to fall for her ever since they had landed in Cairo? She had given him plenty of chances but he was too late. It was no use him taking a definite interest now.

They flew over arid desert land and even saw a camel train.

"I thought they no longer existed," said Romy getting out her camera.

"Everything still goes on if you know

where to look for it," said the sheik. "You remember my telling you about the desert?"

She nodded. "I'll never forget."

"Well, have you had any further thoughts about it?"

She was quiet for a moment. "Yes, I'm willing to believe there is something spiritual about it. And I can see the tranquillity of it from up here, but I must admit when I was lost I was very frightened."

"You wouldn't be human if you hadn't been."

They landed in Alexandria some time after noon. From the air it seemed a big sprawling built-up mass.

"It *is* the second largest city in Egypt," said Martin.

Romy stared at him and he admitted, "I read that in the guide book."

"And it boasts eight million people," added the sheik. "But let's not waste our time on statistics."

He led them to Cecil Hotel where they had a late lunch in a restaurant overlooking the sea.

Abu Ben pointed out to them the castle which now stood on the site of one of the seven wonders of the world — the Pharos lighthouse. "The only wonder left is in my country," he said proudly.

"And what is that?" asked Decima.

"Why, the pyramids, my dear," he replied.

Everybody laughed, but Decima shrugged, not knowing how ignorant she had sounded.

Afterwards they went on a boat trip to the island of Pharos, passing the yacht club and dilapidated buildings gaily flying lines of washing.

"Isn't it pretty?" said Romy gazing at the brightly coloured fishing boats bobbing about and nets drying on the shore. She clung to Martin's arm as they stood in the bows with the spindrift in their faces.

"Yeah." He gave her arm a squeeze. "Let's lose this crowd when we get back to terra firma."

She looked at him sharply, unable to believe he had said that.

Somehow it was amusing seeing him struggling, unaware that it was all for nothing.

She turned to him and said, "I'm afraid I've promised to go souvenir-hunting with Sharon." She babbled on, "I haven't got half the stuff I wanted. I promised my little cousin a plaque of the Sphinx."

He shrugged good-naturedly. "Okay."

He was too nice if that were possible. She couldn't imagine Shane giving up so easily.

Shane!

She frowned. What did he think he was doing performing his own stunts? She recalled the strange icy feeling she'd had when she had learnt what was going on. She gave a deep shudder. Supposing, just supposing Alex had got him there under false pretences, making out there was a scene that needed re-shooting, then offered to let him do a stunt. It could be dangerous.

And the film crew wouldn't know until it was too late.

She couldn't bear to think that anything had happened to Shane.

Another thought struck her. Alex could have dismissed the crew, the same as he had dismissed her.

All at once she wanted to get back to Cairo.

But the sheik was talking to Decima and Romy didn't like to interrupt. Just then the boat turned swiftly and sped back to the harbour with them.

"We won't have to leave it too late getting back," said one of the camera crew, to Romy's relief. "We've got a lot of clearing up to do. If we don't get a move on we'll miss the closing-down party."

"Don't worry," said the sheik. "We're going home now."

The flight back to Cairo was uneventful and they were tired, so most of them dozed.

Romy couldn't sleep, she was too worried about Shane. But why was she so concerned about the model? Had she fallen for him? The idea sounded farcical but life without him didn't look very exciting. She would miss him.

Before she knew it they were coming in to land in the palace grounds where they were surprised and overjoyed to see Kieron, fully recovered from his camel bite, waiting for them.

There followed tearful farewells with the sheik and Tanita. They had all got on famously together in the short time they had known each other and it was possible they would never meet again.

Tanita clung to Romy as if she could never bear to let her go and Romy hugged her tightly.

The sheik looked serious. "I shall never forget you, Romy, and what you did. Any time you are in trouble, God forbid, I hope you will always remember we are your friends."

She was too choked to reply.

They left the palace at last and Romy remembered Shane. He wasn't at the hotel when they got there and the receptionist said she hadn't seen him.

Now Romy was really worried. She asked Martin to accompany her to the set.

"Surely they've dismantled that by now," he said, as they went to ask the doorman to get them a taxi. "We're flying home tomorrow. Is it important? I thought you wanted to buy souvenirs with Sharon."

"I can't explain. It's just a gut feeling I have. Bear with me, Martin."

The first person they saw when they arrived at the site of the set, now non-existent, was Shane.

Romy flew into his arms. "Oh, what a relief," she said, laughing and crying at the same time. "I thought you were . . . "

Shane took advantage of the situation and kissed her, a lingering kiss that sent a spasm of joy rocketing down to her toes and back again.

"Well, I'll make myself scarce," murmured Martin but neither of them heard.

Shane let Romy go but kept his arms loosely around her as his eyes searched hers. In that moment she knew for certain! That look confirmed it. She loved him. She loved Shane Shelley.

Would he propose again? She doubted it. Why should he, after Last time?

And yet . . . from the way he was looking at her . . .

"What brought that on?" he asked as they went in search of a taxi. He hastened to add, "Not that I'm complaining, mind."

"I thought you'd been killed doing a stunt."

"I told you!" He handed her in. "I want to do my own stunts from now on and Alex let me try. Actually you were right. I did do the death-defying leap." He saw her expression of alarm. "It was all right. I was brilliant."

"If you say so," she murmured.

As the hotel loomed before them, he asked teasingly, "Were you really worried?"

"Of course I was!"

"Well, we won't concern ourselves about that now." His eyes sparkled like dark emeralds. "We've got to get ready for the party."

He seized her arm and turned her to face a mirror behind the reception desk. "Look at that woman."

She looked and saw a woman in love gazing back at her. Yes it was her. She had to be honest with herself now. She felt sure this feeling wasn't a fluke, it must have been building up inside her brain all this time and she hadn't noticed it. All of a sudden she knew — she wanted to marry Shane!

Oh no, she'd really flipped now. Where was that girl who didn't need a man to make her happy? She was going back on all her principals.

She laughed to cover up the melancholy in her heart. She might never see him again. She was scheduled to work in London next and he had told her he was going to do a modelling job in South Africa. She wasn't the kind of girl to enjoy one-night stands so there was no future for them. It looked like it was to be marriage or nothing. How unfair. she'd just found him and now she was going to lose him. What a cruel world it was.

He took her hands in his and raised them to his lips to kiss the tips one by one.

"I've been most remiss, my dear." His green eyes were gazing boldly at her but with a hint of amusement. "I wondered what I'd forgotten. I knew there was something."

What could it be he'd forgotten? Perhaps he was thinking of asking for a one-night stand after all and if that was what he wanted, so be it. It wouldn't be the same though . . .

"Darling, will you marry me? We could announce it at the party."

He hadn't forgotten, she decided, he was deliberately tormenting her. Well, two could play at that game.

She hid a grin and said, "I'll think about it."

"Oh Romy . . . " He sounded so crestfallen.

"You are an idiot," she whispered, pushing her fingers into his dense dark hair. "I've thought and the answer is yes."

THE END

Other titles in the Linford Romance Library:

A YOUNG MAN'S FANCY
Nancy Bell

Six people get together for reasons of their own, and the result is one of misunderstanding, suspicion and mounting tension.

THE WISDOM OF LOVE
Janey Blair

Barbie meets Louis and receives flattering proposals, but her reawakened affection for Jonah develops into an overwhelming passion.

MIRAGE IN THE MOONLIGHT
Mandy Brown

En route to an island to be secretary to a multi-millionaire, Heather's stubborn loyalty to her former flatmate plunges her into a grim hazard.

WITH SOMEBODY ELSE
Theresa Charles

Rosamond sets off for Cornwall with Hugo to meet his family, blissfully unaware of the shocks in store for her.

A SUMMER FOR STRANGERS
Claire Hamilton

Because she had lost her job, her flat and she had no money, Tabitha agreed to pose as Adam's future wife although she believed the scheme to be deceitful and cruel.

VILLA OF SINGING WATER
Angela Petron

The disquieting incidents that occurred at the Vatican and the Colosseum did not trouble Jan at first, but then they became increasingly unpleasant and alarming.